Text Book Of

PHARMACEUTICAL ANALYSIS I

For

First Year B. Pharmacy
Semester II

As Per Syllabus of Savitribai Phule Pune University

Ms. Vandana Gawande

M. Pharm, Quality Assurance Techniques
Asst. Professor,
Sinhgad Institute of Pharmacy,
Narhe, Pune – 411041, Maharashtra.

NIRALI
PRAKASHAN
ADVANCEMENT OF KNOWLEDGE

N1315

Pharmaceutical Analysis I   **ISBN 978-93-5164-531-3**

Second Edition : January 2016

© : Author

Published By :

NIRALI PRAKASHAN

Abhyudaya Pragati, 1312, Shivaji Nagar,
Off J.M. Road, PUNE – 411005
Tel - (020) 25512336/37/39, Fax - (020) 25511379
Email : niralipune@pragationline.com

☞ DISTRIBUTION CENTRES

PUNE

Nirali Prakashan : 119, Budhwar Peth, Jogeshwari Mandir Lane, Pune 411002, Maharashtra
Tel : (020) 2445 2044, 66022708, Fax : (020) 2445 1538
Email : bookorder@pragationline.com, niralilocal@pragationline.com

Nirali Prakashan : S. No. 28/27, Dhyari, Near Pari Company, Pune 411041
Tel : (020) 24690204 Fax : (020) 24690316
Email : dhyari@pragationline.com, bookorder@pragationline.com

MUMBAI

Nirali Prakashan : 385, S.V.P. Road, Rasdhara Co-op. Hsg. Society Ltd.,
Girgaum, Mumbai 400004, Maharashtra
Tel : (022) 2385 6339 / 2386 9976, Fax : (022) 2386 9976
Email : niralimumbai@pragationline.com

☞ DISTRIBUTION BRANCHES

JALGAON

Nirali Prakashan : 34, V. V. Golani Market, Navi Peth, Jalgaon 425001,
Maharashtra, Tel : (0257) 222 0395, Mob : 94234 91860

KOLHAPUR

Nirali Prakashan : New Mahadvar Road, Kedar Plaza, 1st Floor Opp. IDBI Bank
Kolhapur 416 012, Maharashtra. Mob : 9850046155

NAGPUR

Pratibha Book Distributors : Above Maratha Mandir, Shop No. 3, First Floor,
Rani Jhanshi Square, Sitabuldi, Nagpur 440012, Maharashtra
Tel : (0712) 254 7129

DELHI

Nirali Prakashan : 4593/21, Basement, Aggarwal Lane 15, Ansari Road, Daryaganj
Near Times of India Building, New Delhi 110002
Mob : 08505972553

BENGALURU

Pragati Book House : House No. 1, Sanjeevappa Lane, Avenue Road Cross,
Opp. Rice Church, Bengaluru – 560002.
Tel : (080) 64513344, 64513355,Mob : 9880582331, 9845021552
Email:bharatsavla@yahoo.com

CHENNAI

Pragati Books : 9/1, Montieth Road, Behind Taas Mahal, Egmore,
Chennai 600008 Tamil Nadu, Tel : (044) 6518 3535,
Mob : 94440 01782 / 98450 21552 / 98805 82331,
Email : bharatsavla@yahoo.com

niralipune@pragationline.com | www.pragationline.com

Also find us on 🆕 www.facebook.com/niralibooks

Acknowledgement ...

I express sincere and whole hearted gratitude towards Dr. K. G. Bothara (Principal, Sinhgad Institute of Pharmacy, Narhe), it is because of his constant support and encouragement work for this was book started. My own teachers Dr. M. C. Damle, Dr. S. V. Gandhi, Mrs. M. V. Dhoka who developed interest in me towards this subject during my graduation and post graduation years must be specially mentioned on this occasion. My co-workers, especially Swapnila, Swati Mam, Shalaka Mam, Titiksh, Amol Sir, Pankaj Sir, Anand Sir, Balu Sir and Pramod Sir for trusting me and supporting me in my ups and downs. My gratitude extends to my students Swati Saxena, Deepak Shelke, Supriya Deshmukh, Poonam Harpale, for helping in proof reading this book from student point of view.

I am thankful to Nirali Prakashan for giving me opportunity to write with them, especially Mr. Jignesh Furia, Dr. S. B. Gokhale, Mr. Malik Shaikh (DTP), Mrs. Anjali Muley (Figure Artist), Mr. Ravindra Walodre (Graphics Designer) for their timely support.

It would not have been possible without blessings of god almighty, my parents and family members who were there standing beside me throughout my career and in writing this book.

Date: 28th March 2015   **Vandana Gawande**

Preface ...

It gives me immense pleasure to keep first edition of this book in front of you. With this book I would like to welcome pharmacy students to the fascinating world of analytical chemistry. This book aims to be a starting point for pharmacy students to develop interest and clear basic concepts involved in analytical chemistry. It is structured exactly as per syllabus of Savitribal Phule Pune University and contents are covered in the simple language. With the advent of sophisticated analytical instruments although modern techniques have replaced volumetric and gravimetric techniqes, with the knowledge of basic and fundamental principles contained in this book students will be able to step on systematic study of modern analytical chemistry as preparation of definate molar solutions is integral part of any analysis, even statitstical data obtained is meaningless without its correct interpretation.

Suggestions for improvement in the book are welcome and will be taken care of in the next editions. I sincerely aplogize for mistakes if any.

Date: 28th March 2015   Vandana Gawande

Syllabus ...

S. P. Pune University syllabus
PHARMACEUTICAL ANALYSIS I (Theory)

Hours: 45   **Marks: 70**

Sr. No.	Topic	Hours.
1.	**Introduction to Analytical Chemistry** Review of Fundamental Aspects-Qualitative, Quantitative Analysis, Types of Quantitative Analysis, Normality, Molarity, Molality, Mole Fraction, Molecular Weight, Equivalent Weight, Expression of Concentration and Strength of Solution, Primary and Secondary Standards	04
2.	**Introduction to Statistical Treatment of Analytical Data** Accuracy and Precision, Errors and their Types, Significant Figures, Standard Deviation, Confidence Limit, Test of Significance, Rejection of a Result, Correlation Coefficient and Coefficient of Determination.	03
3.	**Acid Base Titration** Theories, Acid - Base Equilibria in Water, the pH Scale, Distribution of Acid-base Species with pH, Weak Acids and Bases, Salts of Weak Acids and Bases, Buffers, Polyprotic Acids and their Salts. Acid Base Titration Curves for Strong Acid-strong Base Titration, Weak Acid-strong Base Titration, Weak Base - Strong Acid Titration, Titration of Polyfunctional Acids and Bases, Acid - Base Indicators, Titration of Amino Acid.	10
4.	**Non-aqueous Acid Base Titration** Dissociating and Non-dissociating Solvents, Acid-base Character, Leveling and Differentiating Effects, Solvents, Titrants and Indicators used in Determination of Acids and Bases.	03
5.	**Precipitation Reactions and Titration** Solubility of Slightly Soluble Salts, Solubility Product, Effect of pH, Temperature and Solvent on Solubility of Salts, Common Ion Effect, Calculation of Titration Curves, Indicators Used, Argentometric Titration and Titration involving Ammonium and Potassium Thiocyanate, Mohr's Method, Volhard's Method and Fajan's Method.	06
6.	**Complexometric Reactions and Titration** Complexes and Stability Constants, Chelates, Metal-EDTA Titration Curves, Metal Indicators, Types of Complexometric Titration.	05
7.	**Oxidation - Reduction Reactions and Titration** Half Reactions, Nernst Equation, Redox Equivalent Weights, Redox Indicators, Titration with Potassium Permanganate, Ceriometry, Potassium Dichromate, Iodine, Periodic Acid, Potassium Bromate Titration, Sodium Nitrite Titration, Titanious Chloride Titration.	10
8.	**Gravimetric Methods** Principles, Formation and Properties of Precipitates, Unit Operations in Gravimetry, Organic Precipitants.	04

***

Contents ...

***

1

INTRODUCTION TO ANALYTICAL CHEMISTRY

1.1 Review of Fundamental Aspects

1.2 Types of Analytical Methods

1.3 Expression of Concentration and Strength of Solution

1.4 Primary and Secondary Standards

1.5 Relevance and Significance of Analytical Chemistry to Pharmaceutical Sciences

1.1 REVIEW OF FUNDAMENTAL ASPECTS

Analysis is the process/method of studying the nature of any material or determining its essential features/constituents by separating its constituent elements.

Hence, **analytical chemistry** deals with intentionally produced decomposition or separation of materials into their ingredients or elements so as to find their nature or quantity.

Qualitative analysis gives information about identity of atomic/molecular species/functional groups in the sample. In other words, it deals with 'what' is present in the sample.

Quantitative analysis gives numerical information in the form of relative amount of one or more constituents present in the sample or sample as a whole. Hence, it deals with 'how much' is present in the sample.

1.2 TYPES OF ANALYTICAL METHODS

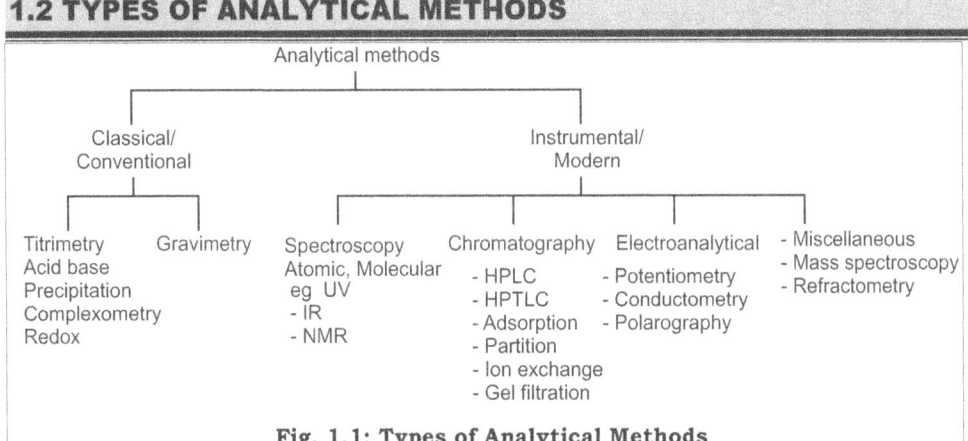

Fig. 1.1: Types of Analytical Methods

Table 1.1: Comparison of Classical and Instrumental Methods

Classical	Instrumental
1. These are crude/conventional methods of analysis performed at the preliminary stages of research.	1. These make use of sophisticated instruments and are used at the advanced stages of research to draw important conclusions.
2. Accuracy is limited.	2. Accuracy varies with the technique but certainly greater than classical methods.
3. These rely on chemical reactions and measured quantities like mass, volume.	3. These are based on physical and chemical properties of sample under influence of energies such as light, magnetic field, potential, etc.
4. They are usually specific for particular class of substance hence do not require complex pretreatment e.g. Assay of sulphamethoxazole from co-trimoxazole tablets IP.	4. They are responsive to variety of constituents present in the sample, hence sample pretreatment is always needed. e.g. Assay of trimethoprim from co-trimoxazole tablets IP.
5. These are not very sensitive, larger quantities of samples are required [few milligrams].	5. Majority of the methods are extremely sensitive, capable of analysing micrograms and nanograms of substance.

Classical	Instrumental
6. Procedures are simple to be carried out in labarotary. Time of analysis is comparatively large.	6. Sound technical knowledge and skills are required to perform these methods. Time of analysis is comparatively short.
7. Cost of analysis is low. Apparatus involved is simple.	7. Cost is comparatively higher depending on instrument. Majority of the instruments require power supply, computer aided data acquisition softwares.

Out of numerous analytical methods available; choice of appropriate method depends on the following factors

1. Level of accuracy and precision needed.
2. Available quantity of sample.
3. Expected concentration of the analyte in sample i.e. sensitivity required.
4. Nature of the matrix in which sample is present [plasma, dosage form].
5. State of the sample [solid, liquid, semisolid].
6. Time and money available.
7. Number of samples to be analysed.

1.3 EXPRESSION OF CONCENTRATION AND STRENGTH OF SOLUTION

At every stage of analysis, it is important to express the concentration of sample, standard, reagent solutions and solvents. Selecting an appropriate unit of concentration helps in keeping clarity of the reaction, allows easy interpretation of the results, helps to decide further scheme of dilution and quantities to be taken in the experiment.

Knowledge of basic elemental terminologies helps in understanding various units of strength.

1. Atomic weight/Atomic mass

It is a relative concept. It is mass of one atom of the element compared with the mass of one atom of hydrogen as one unit. It is defined as one twelfth of the mass of an unbound neutral atom of carbon. It is approximate mass of one nucleus. It is expressed in atomic mass units (amu).

$$1 \text{ amu} = 1.66 \times 10^{-24} \text{ grams}$$

2.   Molecular weight/Molecular mass/Molar mass

It is the mass of a molecule. As per IUPAC it is defined as the ratio of the average mass per formula unit of a substance to $1/12^{th}$ of the mass of an atom of nuclide ^{12}C. In simple words, it is the sum of atomic weights of every atom in the molecule.

It is calculated as the sum of the mass of each constituent atom multiplied by the number of atoms of that element in the molecular formula.

e.g. $KMnO_4$ has molecular weight is 158.

Atom	Mass	Number of atoms	Total mass
K	39.1	1	39.1
Mn	54.9	1	54.9
O	16	4	64.0
			$\Sigma = 158$

It is expressed in Daltons, atomic units, g/mol.

Table 1.2: Atomic weights of common elements

Atom	Symbol	Atomic weight	Valency
Hydrogen	H	1.0	1
Bromine	Br	79.9	1
Calcium	Ca	40.1	2
Carbon	C	12.0	4
Chlorine	Cl	35.5	1
Iron	Fe	55.8	2
Oxygen	O	16.0	2
Nitrogen	N	14.0	3
Potassium	K	39.1	1

3. Equivalent weight

It is defined as the number of parts by mass of the element which can displace or combine with 1.008 parts by mass of hydrogen or 8 parts by mass of oxygen or 35.46 parts by mass of chlorine or one equivalent mass of any other element.

It is relative number and does not have units but it can be expressed in grams known as gram equivalent weight.

It is calculated by dividing molecular weight by valency. Valency or equivalence factor (e.f.) differs by the nature of reaction the substance undergoes.

1. For acids, valency is number of replaceable hydrogen atoms present in one mole of acid.

    For HCl, valency is one, so equivalent weight = $\dfrac{\text{Molecular weight}}{1}$

    For H_2SO_4, valency or e.f. is two, so equivalent weight = $\dfrac{\text{Molecular weight}}{2}$

2. For bases, valency is the number of replaceable hydroxyl ions present in one mole of base or number of hydrogen ions base is capable of accepting.

    e.g. NaOH valency is one, equivalent weight = Molecular weight.

3. For oxidizing and reducing agents, valency is the number of electrons accepted or lost in a particular reaction.

    e.g. For $KMnO_4$

    $KMnO_4 + 8H^+ + 5e^- \rightarrow Mn^{2+} + 4H_2O$

    Equivalent weight = $\dfrac{\text{Molecular weight}}{5}$

4. For precipitation reaction, number of ions which will precipitate in a given reaction. e.g. for $AgNO_3$

    e.g. $AgNO_3 + Cl^- \rightarrow AgCl\downarrow$ Equivalent weight = Molecular weight

There are several ways of expressing concentration.

1. Percentage by mass (M) or volume (V)

2. Parts per solvent

3. Molarity

4. Molality

5. Normality

6. Mole-fraction.

1. Percentage by mass (M) or volume (V)

Percentage by mass is defined as the number of grams of solute present in 100 parts (gm or ml) of solution. It can be either mass/mass, mass/volume or volume/volume.

Accordingly units like %weight (gm)/100 volume (ml), and terminologies like w/w, w/v, v/v are used.

e.g. 2% w/v solution of sucrose in water is prepared by dissolving 2 gm of sucrose in 100 ml of water.

Term used	Meaning	Abbreviation	Unit
Mass fraction	% weight/weight	% w/w	g/g
Mass concentration	% weight/volume	% w/v	g/ml
Volume concentration	% volume/volume	% v/v	ml/ml

It can also be expressed in terms of gm/ml, mg/ml, µg/ml etc.

2. Parts per solvent

Parts per million (ppm) is equivalent to µg/ml or mg/L e.g. 10 ppm means 10 µg of a substance is present in one ml of solution or 10 mg is present in one litre. Unit of weight is one million times smaller than unit of volume.

Percentage and parts per solvent are easier ways of expressing concentration and do not require knowledge of molecular weight of substances. Unknown solutions can be easily expressed.

Similarly, ppb is parts per billion, it is equivalent to 1 mg/1000L or 1 µg/L.

ppb is 1000 times smaller than ppm. Unit of weight is billion times smaller than unit of volume. Rarely parts per trillion (ppt) is used.

3. Molarity (M)

Molarity is the number of moles of solute present in 1000 ml or one litre of solution.

One molar [1M] solution is the solution containing one mole of substance in 1000 ml of solution. It has unit mol/L.

$$\text{Molarity (M)} = \frac{\text{Mass of solute} \times 1000}{\text{Molecular weight of solute} \times \text{Volume of solution}}$$

One molar solution is prepared by dissolving one gram molecular weight [molecular weight expressed in grams] in 1000 ml of solution.

4. Molality (m)

Molality is the number of moles of solute present in 1000 g or 1 kg of solvent.

$$\text{Molality (m)} = \frac{\text{Mass of solute} \times 1000}{\text{Molecular mass of solute} \times \text{Mass of solvent}}$$

One molal solution is prepared by dissolving one gram molecular weight in 1000 gm of solution. It has unit mol/kg.

It is less common in analytical chemistry and knowledge about density is necessary to calculate it. It is used in colligative properties like boiling point elevation, freezing point depression where there is change in volume of solution with change in temperature.

5. Normality (N)

Normality is the number of gram equivalents of solute present in 1000 ml of solution.

One normal solution is the solution which contains one gram equivalent of solute in 1000 ml of solution. Depending on type of reaction, equivalent weight changes for the substance. It has unit equivalent/L.

$$\text{Normality(N)} = \frac{\text{Mass of solute} \times 1000}{\text{Equivalent weight of solute} \times \text{Volume of solution}}$$

One normal solution may or may not be equivalent to one molar solution. They can be related and interconverted to each other by following.

$$\text{Molarity} \times \text{Molecular weight} = \text{Normality} \times \text{Equivalent weight}$$

$$\text{Normality} = \text{Molarity/Equivalent factor}$$

Molarity and normality can be expressed as decimolar (0.1 M), decinormal (0.1 N), millimolar 10^{-3} M or 0.001 M, micromolar (10^{-4} M) as per convenience of analyst. They are largely used for expressing strengths of volumetric reagents used in titrations.

6. Mole-fraction (X)

For solvents (X_1), mole fraction is the ratio between number of moles of solvent (n_1) and total number of moles of solute (n_2) and solvent (n_1) present in solution.

$$X_1 = \frac{\text{Number of moles of solvent}}{\text{Total number of moles present in solution}}$$

$$= \frac{n_1}{n_1 + n_2}$$

Similarly, for solute (X_2), it is

$$X_2 = \frac{\text{Number of moles of solute}}{\text{Total number of moles present in solution}} = \frac{n_2}{n_1 + n_2}$$

In both the cases,

$$\text{Number of moles} = \frac{\text{Mass in gram}}{\text{Molecular weight}}$$

Mole fraction is largely used to know concentration of species undergoing a chemical reaction like titration where there is continuous change in its concentration.

1.4 PRIMARY AND SECONDARY STANDARDS

The term 'standard' indicates a material containing a substance of interest with a known concentration and purity. This concentration and purity is expressed with definite numbers and appropriate units.

By use of standards we can assess functioning of a system [calibration of instruments] or find out concentration of that substance in a new material (assay) or concentration of the material with which it is capable of reacting [standardisation of titrants]. They are also termed as reference standards.

Following are the types of standards –

1.   Primary standards

These are substances which when dissolved in solvent gives solution of definite concentration. They have following properties.

(i)   Extremely pure [99.98%].

(ii)   Highly stable [to oxygen, heat, water].

(iii)   Anhydrous/less hygroscopic [do not absorb water from atmosphere].

(iv)   High molecular weight and easily weighable.

(v)   Preferably non-toxic, safe to handle.

(vi)   Easily available and ready to use.

(vii)   Economic.

(viii) Readily soluble in commonly used solvents.

They are maintained by organisations/national laboratories. They are used to calibrate/certify/standardise secondary standards.

e.g. Anhydrous Na_2CO_3 for standardisation of HCl, Potassium hydrogen phthalate for standardisation of perchloric acid and NaOH.

For preparing primary standard solutions one must use solvents of high grade purity.

2.   Secondary standards

These are the reagents which do not meet criteria for primary standards but are required in analysis. These must be standardised by using primary standards.

e.g. NaOH is Hygroscopic and contains impurities of NaCl, Na_2CO_3 and Na_2SO_4.

It is less pure than primary standards but is chemically stable and fit to be used as a standard. Potassium permanganate is another example of secondary standard. It is unstable and it is unsuitable for being used as primary standard. It is standardised against sodium thiosulphate, oxalic acid and arsenic trioxide.

Secondary standards are involved in actual analysis of unknown samples e.g. NaOH is used to assay aceclofenac by potentiometric titration.

In preparation of standard solution one should use pure, deionised solvent to keep the quality of standard intact.

Other types of standards are –

1. International standards

These are the materials synthesised to the specifications of an international forum e.g. Pharmacopoeia. They represent the material of highest possible accuracy. They are not available to an ordinary user for purposes of day to day comparisons and calibrations. e.g. Prednisone tablets RS and salicyclic acid Tablets RS from United States Pharmacopoeia specially used for validation of disintegrating and non-disintegrating type dissolution apparatus respectively.

2. Working standards

These are high purity standards commercially available and duly certified against primary or secondary standards. Working standards are very widely used for calibrating general laboratory instruments, for comparison measurements or for checking quality of industrial products.

1.5 RELEVANCE AND SIGNIFICANCE OF ANALYTICAL CHEMISTRY TO PHARMACEUTICAL SCIENCES

Pharmaceutical sciences involve all aspects about medicines right from its discovery, approval, synthesis, formulation, stability and distribution to the consumers. Analytical chemistry plays important role in all phases of life of drug majorly for:

1. Identification [Qualitative analysis]

2. Estimation [Quantitative analysis]

3. Separation [Mixture analysis/Purification]

Important Uses of Analytical Techniques

1. Measuring bioavailability of drugs.
2. Purifying drugs during synthesis.
3. Identifying drug metabolic pathways.
4. Assay of drugs from different formulations i.e. dosage forms.
5. Monitoring quality of raw materials, inprocess materials, finished products.
6. Evaluation of stability of drugs to establish shelf life, storage conditions, selection of packaging materials.
7. Monitoring of environmental conditions during manufacturing.
8. Impurity profiling.
9. Identification, knowing elemental composition of unknowns.
10. Structural elucidation/characterisation.
11. Monitoring course of reactions in synthesis.

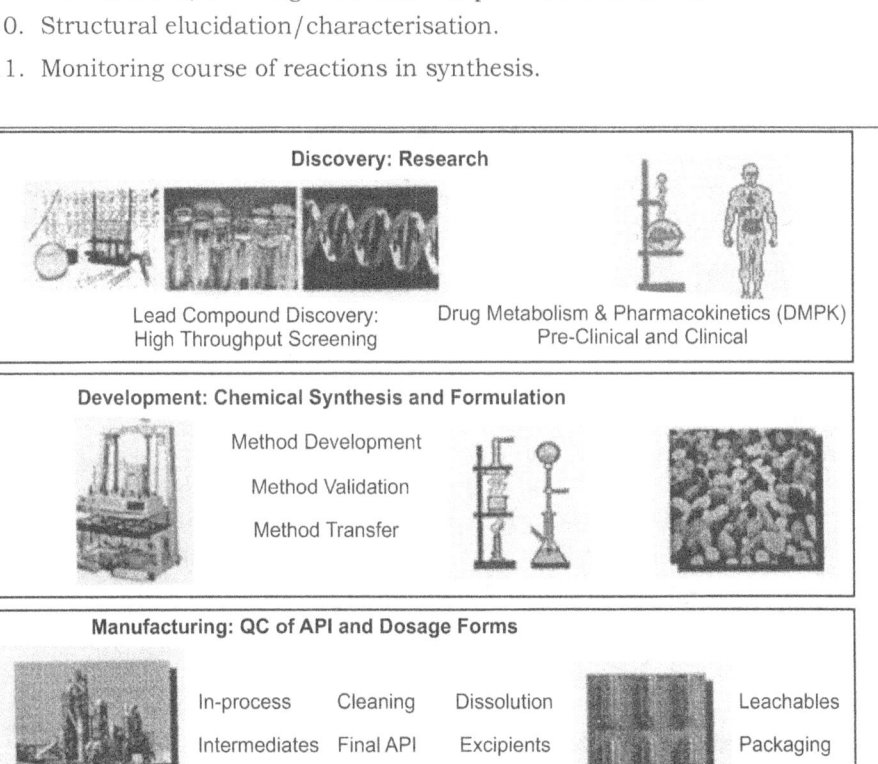

Fig. 1.2: Significance of analytical chemistry in various steps of drug development and manufacturing

Have you heard about him ?

Izaak Maurits (Piet) Kolthoff (February 11, 1894 - March 4, 1993) was a highly influential chemist and is considered as the Father of Modern Analytical Chemistry.

Kolthoff was born in Almelo, Netherlands. In high school, his first chemistry course allowed him to develop a keen interest in the subject. This inspired him to create his own laboratory in his kitchen. Some of his experiments involved generation of hydrogen sulfide gas. In 1911, he went to Utrecht University to study chemistry, but he chose pharmacy to avoid the strict classical language requirement. The main areas of his research were pH, electron transfer, precipitation reactions, voltammetry, emulsion polymerisation induced reactions, compounds containing sulfhydryl and disulfide groups, and non aqueous solutions. As a faculty member at the University of Minnesota from 1927 to 1962, Kolthoff was a world-renowned educator, author of nearly 1,000 papers and numerous textbooks, adviser to more than 50 doctoral chemistry students, and an international leader in advancing analytical chemistry as a modern scientific discipline. He was given this title based on his development of analytical chemistry as a modern science. By applying fundamental physical principles and insights, Kolthoff transformed chemical analysis from a qualitative to a quantitative science. He played an important role in establishing the field as a separate discipline from other areas of chemistry.

"Analytical chemistry, especially in those days, was bare of almost any scientific interpretations. It became clear to me that such an understanding was not only, necessary to increase the prestige of analytical chemistry as a real science by providing these interpretations, but that a good understanding of physical; chemical, and physico-chemical fundamentals would lead to the development of new methods, improvement of existing methods, and to the calculation of errors in analytical procedures".

- I. M. Kolthoff, from a 1973 interview with Robert C. Brasted published in the Journal of Chemical Education (American Chemical Society).

2

INTRODUCTION TO STATISTICAL TREATMENT OF ANALYTICAL DATA

In any field of science, data obtained is treated statistically mainly for two reasons viz. to get better representation for its easy interpretation and to draw important conclusions out of it.

Accuracy, precision, significant figures help to provide validity of the data and aid in accepting/rejecting it.

Tests of significance, correlation, regression helps to represent data in better terms as well as to establish new insights in the results obtained and to draw important conclusions about the data.

2.1 ACCURACY AND PRECISION, STANDARD DEVIATION

Accuracy

As per International Conference on harmonisation (ICH) Q_2 (R_1) guidelines accuracy of an analytical procedure is 'closeness of agreement between the value which is accepted either as a conventional true value or an accepted reference value and the value found'.

It should be established across the specified range of the analytical procedure.

Accuracy can either be assessed by applying the procedure to reference standard/synthetic mixtures of the drug product spiked with drug substance or drug product spiked with known amounts of impurities or by comparing the results obtained by another already validated method.

- Minimum 9 determinations over minimum of 3 concentration levels shall be done.

- It is expressed as percent recovery calculated as assay of known added amount of analyte in the sample or by following formula.

$$\text{Percent error} = \frac{|\text{measured value} - \text{Accepted value}|}{\text{Accepted value}} \times 100$$

As difference is normalised, % error is always positive. It shall be reported with confidence interval.

Precision

According to ICH, it is closeness of agreement [degree of scatter] between a series of measurements obtained from multiple sampling of the same homogeneous sample under the prescribed conditions.

- It shall be determined by assaying different aliquots of a homogeneous sample. Independent analysis of the samples have to be carried out through complete analytical procedure from sample preparation to final test result.

- Minimum 9 determinations covering the specified range over 3 concentrations or minimum 6 determinations at 100% of test concentration shall be done.

- It is expressed in terms of standard deviation (S.D.) and percent relative standard deviation (RSD) with confidence interval.

  It can be considered at 3 levels.

1. Repeatability [Intra assay precision]

   Precision under the same operating conditions over a short interval of time.

2. Intermediate precision

   It expresses variations within laboratories like different days, different analysts, different equipments in the same laboratory.

3. Reproducibility

   It expresses precision between laboratories. It is usually applied to standardisation of methodology.

Standard Deviation

It is the measure of dispersion of the data and denoted by symbol 'σ' (sigma). It is defined as the positive square root of the mean square deviation of the variables measured from mean. It has no unit.

$$\text{S.D.} = \sqrt{\frac{\Sigma (x - \bar{x})^2}{n}}$$

where,   x = Variables

$\bar{x}$ = Mean

n = Number of observations

S.D. = $\sqrt{\text{Variance}}$

Steps to calculate S.D.

1. Determine mean of data $(\bar{x})$.

2. Determine difference between each observation and mean $(x - \bar{x})$.

3. Determine square of each difference $(x - \bar{x})^2$.
4. Find variance i.e. average mean variation.

$$\frac{\Sigma (x - \bar{x})^2}{n}$$

5. Determine square root of variance.

Percent Relative Standard Deviation (% RSD)/Coefficient of Variation (CV)

*   It is a measure of relative variation to the mean. If value of % RSD is less, it indicates data is uniform. Larger values of % RSD indicate data is spread.

$$\% \text{ RSD} = \frac{\text{S.D.}}{\text{Mean}} \times 100$$

% RSD not more than 2 is fairly accepted by various regulatory guidelines however smaller values indicate better precision.

e.g. S.D. of 9, 4, 5, 6. Follow these steps.

1. $\bar{x} = 6$

2. From the values, calculate $x - \bar{x}$ and $(x - \bar{x})^2$.

X	$|x - \bar{x}|$	$(x - \bar{x})^2$
9	3	9
4	2	4
5	1	1
6	0	0

3. Variance = 14/4 = 3.5.
4. S.D. = 1.87. (Calculated by the above mentioned formula).
5. $\% \text{ RSD} = \frac{\text{S.D.}}{\bar{x}} \times 100 = \frac{1.871}{6} \times 100 = 31.16$.

Accuracy and precision are two important analytical method validation parameters proposed by ICH and United States Pharmacopeia (USP).

Accuracy and precision can be easily understood by observing how a target is hit. All the times when target was hit close to centre it is considered accurate, while when it was hit close to each other it is considered precise.

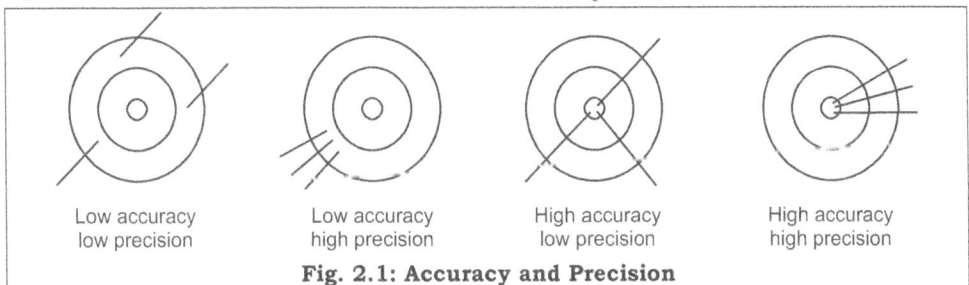

Low accuracy
low precision

Low accuracy
high precision

High accuracy
low precision

High accuracy
high precision

Fig. 2.1: Accuracy and Precision

2.2 CONFIDENCE INTERVAL/CONFIDENCE LIMITS

- It is expressed as a range containing upper and lower values.
- Its an interval of numbers along with a probability that the interval contains the unknown parameter like mean.
- It is always stated with a level of confidence.
- Construction of confidence interval (CI) involves:

  1. Point estimate of the population (usually mean $\bar{x}$).
  2. Level of confidence (as a percentage with corresponding z value).
  3. Standard error of mean [SEM].

  C.I. = Point estimate ± z value × SEM

- z values depend on level of confidence i.e. the probability that confidence interval will contain mean.
- Magnitude of z value increases as the level of confidence increases.

Table 2.1: z values for different confidence levels

Confidence	z value
80%	1.28
90%	1.645
95%	1.96
98%	2.33
99%	2.58
99.8%	3.08
99.9%	3.27

- Standard error of mean (SEM)

$$\text{SEM} = \frac{\text{S.D.}}{\sqrt{n}}$$

S.D. = Standard deviation

n = Number of observations

So at 95% confidence level, confidence interval can be calculated as follows:

$$\text{CI} = \bar{x} \pm 1.96 \text{ SEM}$$

i.e. $\bar{x} - 1.96\,\dfrac{\text{S.D.}}{\sqrt{n}} < \mu < \bar{x} + 1.96\,\dfrac{\text{S.D.}}{\sqrt{n}}$

e.g. for 5 observations, at 95% confidence level, when SEM is 0.33 and $\bar{x}$ is 1.667.

$$\text{CI} = 1.667 - (1.96 \times 0.33) \text{ to } 1.667 + (1.96 \times 0.33)$$
$$= 1.667 - 0.6468 \text{ to } 1.667 + 0.6468$$
$$= 1.0202, 2.3138$$

- We would expect 95 out of 100 intervals shall contain population mean.

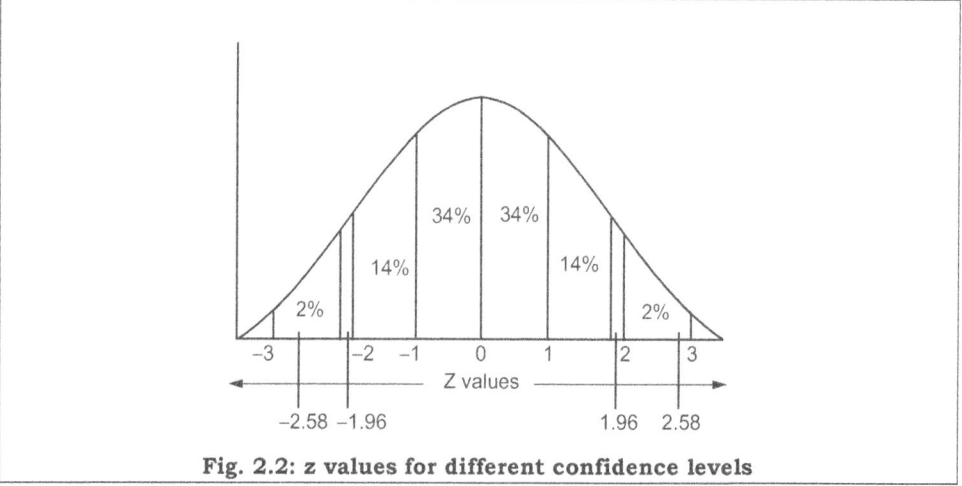

Fig. 2.2: z values for different confidence levels

2.3 ERRORS AND THEIR TYPES

- Error is a difference between a computed, estimated or measured value and the accepted or true value.
- In common language, it refers to a mistake, incorrect or wrong act.
- Because of errors, accuracy and precision of the data decreases and it may become unacceptable.

- There are three types of errors usually encountered in research according to frequency and causes of their occurrence.

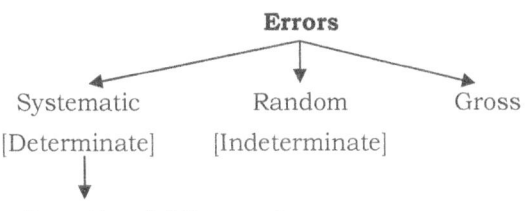

- Operational / Personal
- Instrumental
- Reagent
- Method related

[A] Systematic/Determinate errors

- These are the errors which are direct in nature, their magnitude can be determined and they can be avoided as their origin is known. They cause mean of the data set to differ from accepted value and thus affect accuracy of measurement.

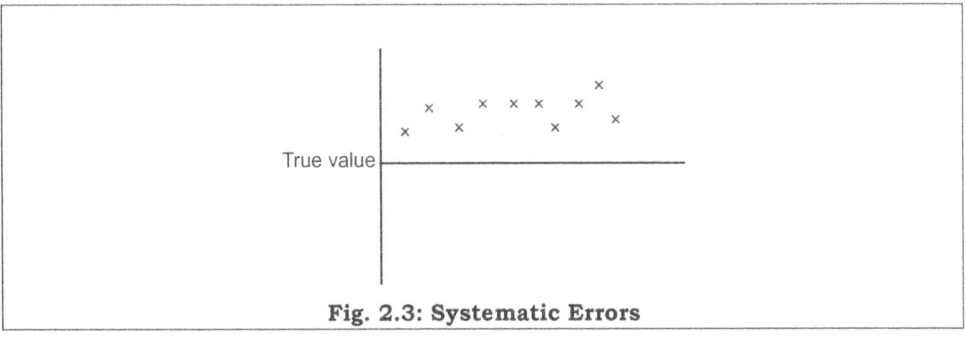

Fig. 2.3: Systematic Errors

- These are the errors which in course of measurements of the same value of given quantity, remains proportional or constant when measurements are made under the same conditions, or vary according to the definite law when conditions change.
- They create characteristic bias in the test results which can be accounted for by applying a correction.

Based on their sources, systematic errors can be further divided as follows:

1. Operational/Personal errors

- These are due to the factors for which the individual analyst is responsible and they are not related to the method or procedure.

- They arise when sound analytical technique is not followed.

  e.g. Incorrect transfer of solutions, incomplete drying of sample before weighing in gravimetry.

- They are mostly due to lack of care or inability of an individual to make certain observations accurately.

  e.g. Improper judging of end point of titration. Improper reading of meniscus of burette.

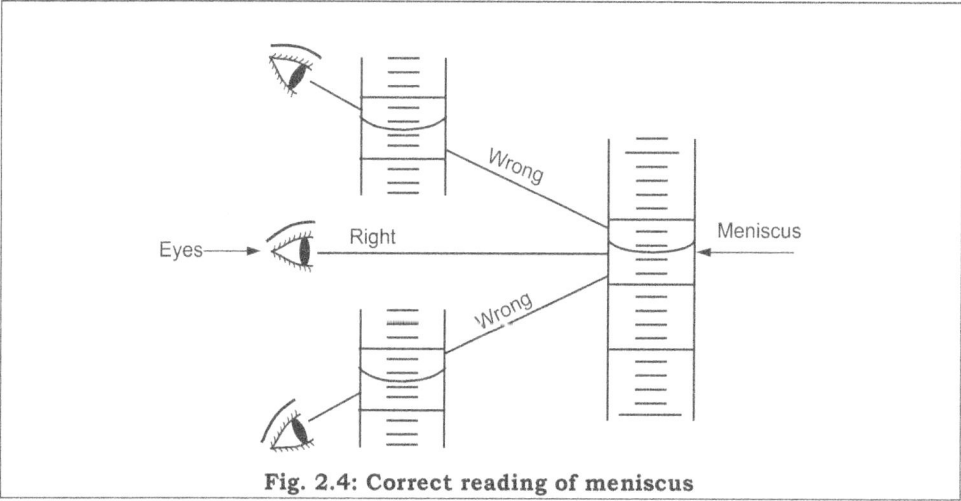

Fig. 2.4: Correct reading of meniscus

2. Instrumental errors

- They are due to faulty construction of instruments, use of uncalibrated/ improperly calibrated instruments and glasswares, improperly maintained glasswares or instruments.

3. Reagent errors

- They are mostly due to use of impure reagents.

- Problems may also arise if reagents are not freshly prepared and if they are not properly stored.

  e.g. Standard solution of perchloric acid must be kept for 24 hours before use for complete reaction of water with acetic anhydride.

  Standard silver nitrate, potassium permanganate solutions must be freshly prepared and used.

- Reagents are available in different grades like laboratory reagent grade, analytical reagent grade, HPLC grade.

- Appropriate grade shall be selected based on type of analysis.

4.   Method related errors

- They are most serious types of errors and are difficult to detect.

- They are present inherently in the method and are significant when appropriate method is not selected.

  e.g. Background absorption in spectroscopic techniques, decomposition on ignition of substance in gravimetry.

[B] Random errors/Indeterminate errors

- Slight variations in the successive measurements made by the same observer with greatest care are random errors.

- These are errors on which analyst has no control and they are incapable of avoiding it.

- Both positive and negative errors may occur and small errors are more frequent than large errors.

- They vary in an unpredictable manner in magnitude and sign. They create a characteristic spread of results for any test method and cannot be accounted for by applying corrections.

  e. g. Errors in pipetting, changes in incubation temperature and period.

- They are minimised by training, supervision and adherence to standard operating procedures.

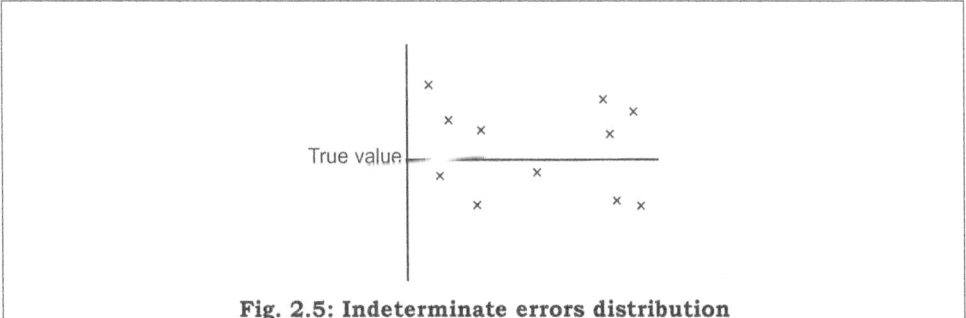

Fig. 2.5: Indeterminate errors distribution

- It causes data to be scattered more or less symmetrically around a mean value and they affect measurement precision.

[C] Gross errors:

- They occur occasionally.

- They are often large and may cause a result to be either high or low.

- They are usually result due to human errors and lead to outliers.

  e.g. addition of completely different reagent because of improper labeling resulting into no reaction or completely different reaction.

General Steps to Prevent/Minimise Errors

- Use of calibrated and validated instruments and glasswares.
- Cleaning of glasswares before and after use.
- Following standard operating procedure, maintaining all necessary conditions.
- Use of pure, freshly prepared reagents.
- Correct labelling of the reagents.
- Training and sound knowledge of the method.

Errors can also be classified as Type I error and Type II error in test of significance.

- When hypothesis is true but we reject it, it is called type I error.
- While type II error means hypothesis is false but we tend to accept it.

Specific steps to reduce systematic errors

1. **Running blank determination**

   This is carrying out separate determination by omitting the sample in same experimental conditions.

   Effect of impurities introduced through reagents and vessels can be eliminated.

2. **Running control determination**

   It is Carrying out separate determination on a reference standard substance under the same experimental conditions. Reference standard should contain same concentration as expected for the sample. Concentration of unknown (x) can be found out by following formula.

   $$X = \frac{\text{Result found for unknown} \times \text{Concentration/Weight of standard}}{\text{Result found for standard}}$$

   Reference standards are available commercially by certain authorities e.g. Bureau of Analysed Samples, National Bureau of Standards.

3. **Use of Independent methods of analysis**

   If two or three methods are available for determination of same constituent, these can be applied and variation can be found out. The best method which gives accurate, reproducible results can be chosen.

   e.g. Determination of strength of HCl by titration with base or precipitation with $AgNO_3$ and weighing AgCl ppt.

4. **Running parallel determinations**

   Here multiple sets of the same experiment are run at a time. It also indicates precision/reproducibility of the result but does not indicate accuracy. However, if same determination is done number of times there should be no great variations.

5. **Standard addition method**

   A known amount of constituent being determined is added to the sample and it is then analysed as a total. The difference between analytical results for samples with and without added constituent gives recovery of method. Also standard addition can be done to a series of concentrations and concentration of unknown can be determined by calibration curve method.

6. **Internal standards**

   Fixed amount of a reference material [internal standard] is added to a series of known concentrations of the material to be measured. The ratio of physical value [peak area] of internal standard and sample is plotted against concentration values. This ratio is called as response factor. Unknown concentration can be determined by extrapolation. Internal standard should be similar to the analyte but it must provide a signal different from analyte.

7. **Amplification methods**

   If determination involves measurement of very small amount of material, reaction of material can be done with a reagent which gives two or more other molecules of measurable material. This increases concentration to be measured or it brings the quantity within scope of apparatus.

8. **Isotopic dilution**

   In this technique known amount of the element being determined, containing a radioactive isotope is mixed with the sample and radioactivity is determined after isolation of that element. It is compared with radioactivity of added element and weight of element is calculated.

2.4 SIGNIFICANT FIGURES/DIGITS

- The significant figures in a measurement includes all the digits that are known plus a last digit that is estimated. i.e. Significant figures = Known + Estimate
- They relate to certainty of a measurement. e.g.

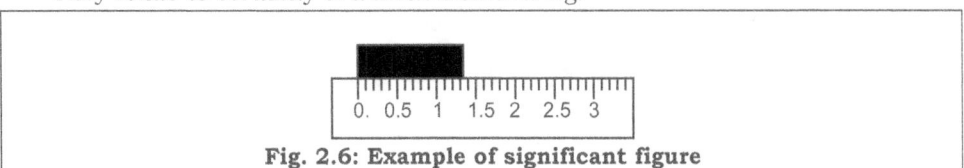

Fig. 2.6: Example of significant figure

- Observation is 1.37 in which 1.3 is known, while 0.07 is unknown/ approximate. Significant figures are total 3. Higher the number of significant more accurate is the measurement.
- There are certain rules governing significant figures.

1. **Rule 1: All digits 1 through 9 are significant**

   e.g.   9,342 = 4 significant figures

   2,33,124 = 6 significant figures

   1.39 = 3 significant figures

   Thus, for an observation containing all the numbers from 1 to 9 (without zero) significant figures equal to the total number of digits.

2. **Rule 2: Zero is significant when it is between two non-zero digits**

   2.06 = 3 significant figures

   Here, '0' is considered as significant figure because it is present between '2' and '6'. Position of decimal point is not considered here.

   206 = 3 significant figures

   1,00,001 = 6 significant figures

   1.00001 = 6 significant figures

3. **Rule 3: Zero right to the decimal point in a number greater than one is significant and it should be counted.**

   10.0 = 3 significant figures

   1.000 = 4 significant figures

   2.00000 = 6 significant figures

   205.0 = 4 significant figures

4. **Rule 4: Zero to the right of decimal point in a number less than one but to the left of non-zero digits is not significant and it should not be counted.**

   0.0013 = 2 significant figures

   0.00103 = 3 significant figures

   0.00024200 = 5 significant figures

   0.001020 = 4 significant figures

5. **Rule 5: Zeros used only to space the decimal point are not significant i.e. zero on the right side of non-zero digits are not considered.**

   1000 = 1 significant figure

   1010 = 3 significant figures

   78,000 = 2 significant figures

Few more examples of significant figures (s.f.)

	Number of s.f.	Rule Number
1235	4	1
2020	3	5
235.0	4	3
0.0270	3	4
235	3	1
0.00010900	5	4
65,100	3	5
19,620,000,000	4	5
102,800	4	5

2.5 CORRELATION AND REGRESSION

Correlation

• It is the statistical technique used to find the relationship between two quantitative variables. Thus, it is used to determine the degree to which two variables are related.

• For example, if we wish to relate number of hours spend in studying to the final grades obtained in the course direct/positive correlation is observed.

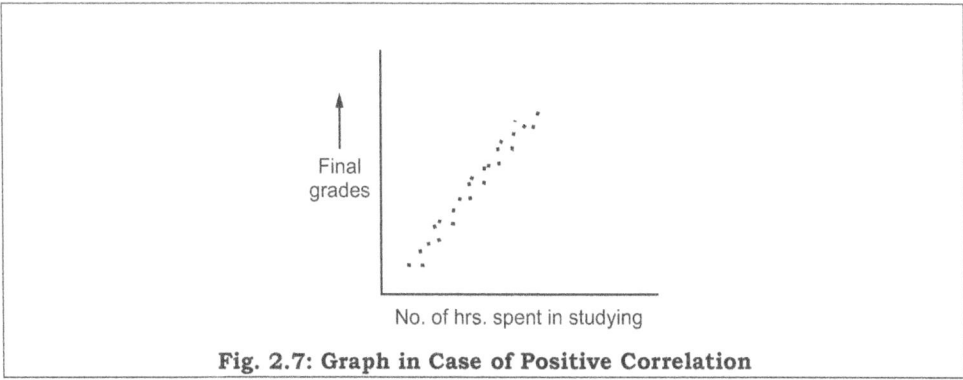

No. of hrs. spent in studying

Fig. 2.7: Graph in Case of Positive Correlation

Positive correlation is observed when quantity of one variable (independent) is increased and it results into increase in quantity of other variable (dependent variable). On the other hand, (indirect) negative correlation is observed when increase in independent variable results in decrease in dependent variable.

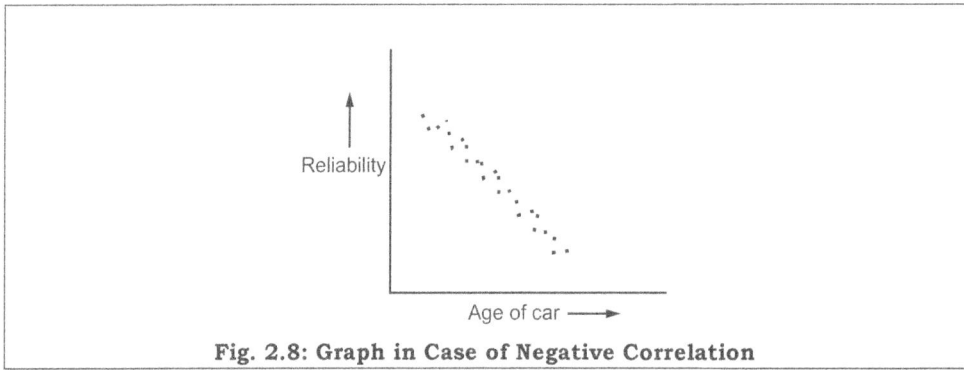

Fig. 2.8: Graph in Case of Negative Correlation

• In pharmaceutical sciences certain variables need to be correlated with each other.

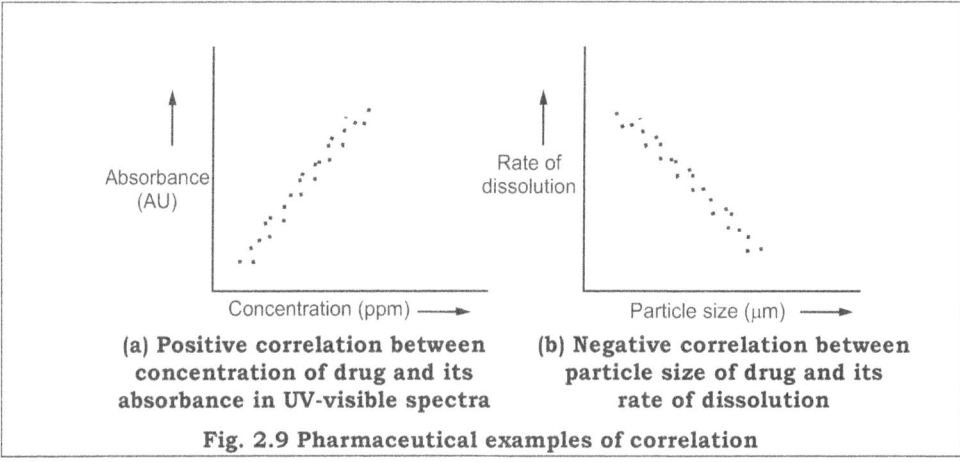

(a) Positive correlation between concentration of drug and its absorbance in UV-visible spectra

(b) Negative correlation between particle size of drug and its rate of dissolution

Fig. 2.9 Pharmaceutical examples of correlation

• There are situations of no correlation when two variables are not related to each other.

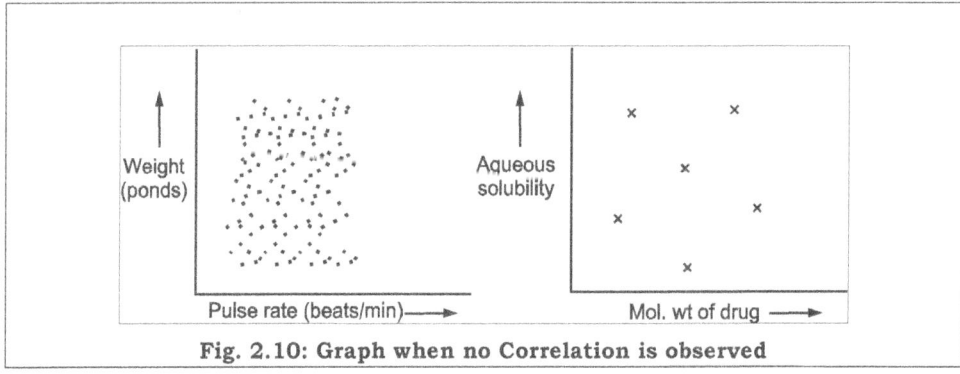

Fig. 2.10: Graph when no Correlation is observed

Correlation Coefficient (r/R)

- It is also called as Pearson's correlation or product moment correlation coefficient.
- It measures the nature and strength between two quantitative variables.
- Its sign (+/−) indicates nature of association.
- Its magnitude (0 − 1) indicates strength of association.
- The value of r ranges between (−1) and (+1).
- It is dimensionless value.

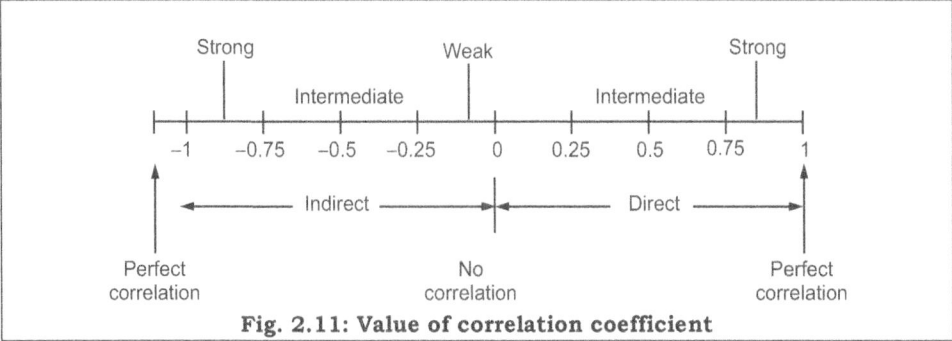

Fig. 2.11: Value of correlation coefficient

$$r = \frac{\Sigma xy - \frac{\Sigma x \Sigma y}{n}}{\sqrt{\left(\Sigma x^2 - \frac{(\Sigma x)^2}{n}\right) \cdot \left(\Sigma y^2 - \frac{(\Sigma y)^2}{n}\right)}}$$

Example:

Sr. No.	Age Years (x)	Weight kg (y)	xy	x^2	y^2
1	7	12	84	49	144
2	6	8	48	36	64
3	8	12	96	64	144
4	5	10	50	25	100
5	6	11	66	36	121
6	9	13	117	81	169
Total	**Σx = 41**	**Σy = 66**	**Σxy = 461**	**Σx² = 291**	**Σy² = 742**

$$r = \frac{461 - \frac{41 \times 66}{6}}{\sqrt{\left(291 - \frac{(41)^2}{6}\right) \cdot \left(742 - \frac{(66)^2}{6}\right)}}$$

r = 0.759 strong direct correlation

Limitations of Correlation Coefficient (r/R)

- Though r measures how closely the two variables are related. It does not validly measures the strength of non-linear relationship.
- Also when sample size (n) is small, r is not reliable.
- Outliers have marked effect on r.

Regression Analysis

- It is the technique concerned with predicting some variable by knowing other variable usually predicting dependent variable (Y) by knowing independent variable (X).
- When X is plotted vs. Y straight line equation can be generated from graph.

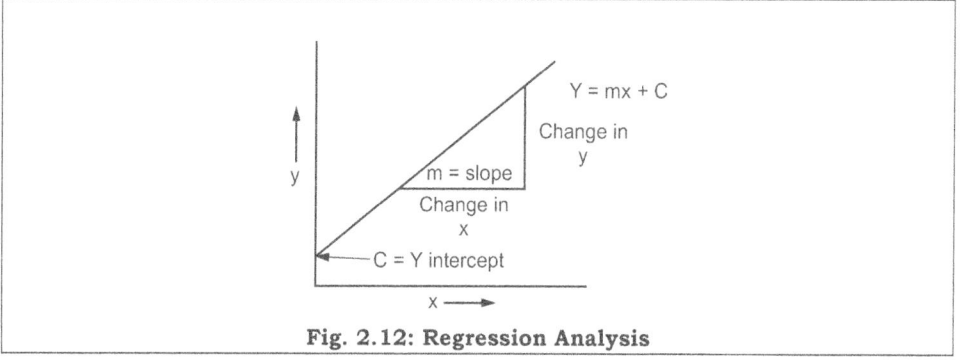

Fig. 2.12: Regression Analysis

- Regression analysis calculates 'best fit' line for a certain set of data. It makes the sum of the squares of the residuals smaller for best fit line than for any other line hence it is also called as least square method.
- If the regression line passes exactly through every point on the scatter plot, it would be able to explain all of the variation. If the line is away from the points, it is less able to explain the variation.

Coefficient of determination (r^2/R^2)

- It is obtained by taking square of correlation coefficient r.
- R^2 values lie between 0 – 1. It is never negative.
- It measures the proportion of total variation in Y which is explained by x.
- It is dimensionless.

  e.g. If r = 0.9, R^2 = 0.81.

  When R^2 is 0.81, it means 81% of the variation in dependent variable is explained by the independent variable. The other 19% variation remains unexplained.

- Correlation and regression forms important part in pharmaceutical sciences. Correlation describes nature of relationship between two variables while regression describes estimation of one variable from other.

- Correlation coefficient represents strength of association while coefficient of determination represents percent of explained variation.

2.6 TESTS OF SIGNIFICANCE, REJECTION OF RESULT

Tests of Significance in Statistics

The statistical procedures used for deciding whether the difference under study is significant or non-significant are called as the test of significance.

Hypothesis is the statement of assumption, Null hypothesis [H₀] is the hypothesis of no difference. It assumes that there is no difference between the hypothetical population and the sample.

Level of Significance: The maximum probability of rejecting the hypothesis is the level of significance. It is denoted by α. e.g. 0.05%, 0.01% etc.

Confidence Interval: The range in which population mean may lie.

Parametric Tests: Tests applied which are based on assumption that the distribution of the population from which the sample has been drawn is normal or Gaussian distribution e.g. 't' test, 'f' test, 'z' test. They assume that population can be fairly estimated from corresponding sample parameters.

These tests fail when population has skewed/non-normal distribution.

Non-parametric Tests: These tests can be applied when sample size is small and there is no normal distribution of the population e.g. Wilcoxon Test, Sign Test, Fisher's Exact Test.

1. F Test/Variance Ratio Test

This test is used to compare the precisions of two sets of data e.g. from two different analytical methods or results from two different laboratories.

F value is calculated and it is compared with table value of 'F'. If the calculated F value is greater than table value then there is significant difference between two sets of data.

$$F = \frac{S_A^2}{S_B^2}$$

'Larger value is taken in numerator'

S = Standard deviation for set A and B

Table values are available with corresponding number of degrees of freedom.

Example for F test

Standard deviation set of 11 observations is $S_A = 0.210$ and $S_B = 0.641$ for set of 13 observations. Is there any significant difference?

$$F = \frac{(0.641)^2}{(0.210)^2} = 9.4$$

Table value : 2.91, 4.71.

Calculated F value is larger than table value and hence data sets are significantly different from each other.

2. Q Test

This test is used to decide acceptance or rejection of outlier. Outlier is the odd observation from the data which is different from the other observations

$$Q = \frac{[\text{Questionable value} - \text{Nearest value}]}{\text{Largest value} - \text{Smallest value}}$$

If the calculated value Q exceeds the table Q value, questionable value may be rejected.

Example for Q test

i)   Determination of cadmium 4.3, 4.1, 4.0, 3.2 µg/g.

Outlier = 3.2

$$Q = \frac{3.2 - 4.0}{4.3 - 3.2} = \frac{0.8}{1.1} = 0.727$$

Table value is 0.831, less than calculated value hence outlier value 3.2 must be retained.

ii) Determination of cadmium 4.3, 4.1, 4.0, 3.2, 4.2, 3.9, 4.0   Outlier = 3.2

$$Q = \frac{3.2 - 3.9}{4.3 - 3.2} = \frac{0.7}{1.1} = 0.63 \qquad \text{Table value} = 0.570$$

Now here, calculated value is greater than table value hence outlier must be rejected.

3. Student 't' test /t test

It is used for comparison of mean of two sets of data or data and true value. Student 't' test is used for small samples. Mean of samples is compared for their significance difference.

$$t = \frac{(\bar{x} - \mu)\sqrt{n}}{S} \text{ or } \frac{(\bar{x}_1 - \bar{x}_2)\sqrt{n}}{\dfrac{S_1 + S_2}{2}}$$

$$\bar{x} = \text{Mean}$$

$$\mu = \text{True value}$$

$$S = \text{Standard deviation}$$

$$n = \text{Number of observations}$$

't' value calculated is compared with table 't' value with corresponding degrees of freedom. If it is greater than table value, their difference is significant and vice-versa.

Table values are also expressed with probability values (P) for confidence in falling 't' value within certain limits. e.g. P – 0.01% t value 3.11, probability of getting 't' value as 3.11 is 1 in 1000 of observations. When 't' test is applied to more sets of samples.

Example for 't' test

1.   Mean of 12 determinations $\bar{x}$ = 8.37.

   True mean μ = 7.91

   S = 0.17

$$t = \frac{(8.37 - 7.91)\sqrt{n}}{0.17} = 9.4$$

Table value is 3.11, less than calculated value hence two sets are significantly different.

Applications of Statistical Tests in Pharmaceutical sciences

They are widely used to compare results of

(a)   Two/more analytical methods for assay of same drug.

   e.g. Assay of paracetamol by Redox titration

   Assay of paracetamol by sodium nitrite titration

(b)   Effect of drug to treat disease from different dosage forms.

   e.g. From tablets, capsules, liquids.

(c)   Effect of different drugs for same disease condition/same effect.

Have you heard about them ?

Sir Francis Galton 1822-1911 Geographer, meteorologist, tropical explorer, inventor of fingerprint identification, eugenicist, cousin of Charles Darwin and best-selling author proposed correlation and regression.

Historians have also suggested that his cousin's lasting fame unfairly overshadowed the substantial scientific contributions Galton made to biology, psychology and applied statistics. Galton's experiment with sweet peas (1875) led to the development of initial concepts of linear regression. In 1875, Galton had distributed packets of sweet pea seeds to seven friends; each friend received seeds of uniform weight but there was substantial variation across different packets. Galton's friends harvested seeds from the new generations of plants and returned them to him. Galton plotted the weights of the daughter seeds against the weights of the mother seeds. Galton realised that the median weights of daughter seeds from a particular size of mother seed approximately described a straight line with positive slope less than 1.0.

Galton aged 87, with Karl Pearson

Karl Pearson (1857-1936) was an influential English mathematician and biometrician. He was also a protege and biographer of Sir Francis Galton.

His Least squares idea was choosing the line that minimises the sum of the squares of the deviations of each observation from the regression line. When the 23-year-old Albert Einstein started a study group, the Olympia Academy, he suggested that the first book to be read was Pearson's *The Grammar of Science*. This book covered several themes that were later became part of the theories of Einstein and other scientists.

I rush from science to philosophy and from philosophy to our old friends the poets and then, over-wearied by too much idealism, I fancy I become practical in returning to science. Have you ever attempted to conceive all there is in the world worth knowing—that not one subject in the universe is unworthy of study? The giants of literature, the mysteries of many-dimensional space, the, attempts Boltzmann and Crookes to penetrate Nature's very laboratory, the Kantian theory of the universe, and the latest discoveries in embryology, with their wonderful tales of the development of life—what an immensity beyond our grasp!
– In his first book, The New Werther.

3

AQUEOUS ACID BASE TITRATION

3.1 DEFINITIONS OF ACIDS AND BASES/THEORIES OF ACIDS AND BASES

1. Arrenius Theory [Radial Theory] [1894]

Acid: Any substance which ionises [partially or completely] in water to give hydrogen ions [H^+]. These ions associate with water to give hydronium ions [H_3O^+]. e.g. HCl.

$$HA \underset{}{\overset{H_2O}{\rightleftharpoons}} H^+ + A^- \underset{}{\overset{H_2O}{\rightleftharpoons}} H_3O^+ + A^-$$

Acid

Base: Any substance which ionises [partially or completely] in water to give hydroxyl ions. e.g. NaOH.

$$BOH \overset{H_2O}{\rightleftharpoons} BH^+ + 2OH^-$$

Pseudo base: They do not contain OH^- ions but tend to increase OH^- concentration of solution. e.g. NH_3.

$$B + H_2O \rightleftharpoons BH^+ + OH^-$$

Limitation

1. Theory is restricted to water as solvent.

2. Not suitable for substances which do not contain H^+/OH^- ions.

3. Acidity is associated with H^+ ion [relatively simple] and basicity is associated with OH^- ion [relatively complex].

2. Lowry and Bronsted Theory [1923]

Acid: Any substance which donates proton $HA \rightleftharpoons H^+ + A^-$

Base: Any substance which accepts proton $B + H^+ \rightleftharpoons BH^+$

Molecules, anions, cations can act as acid and base. After giving proton or accepting it acid base get converted to conjugate base and acids respectively.

Type of ion	**Acids**		**Bases**
e.g. Neutral	$HCl \rightleftharpoons H^+ + Cl^-$		Anion
Cation	$NH_4^+ \rightleftharpoons H^+ + NH_3$		Neutral
Anion	$HCO_3^- \rightleftharpoons H^+ + CO_3^{2-}$		Anion
Cation	$Al(H_2O_4)_6^{3+} \rightleftharpoons H^+ + Al(H_2O_5)_5^{2+}$		cation

Acid always has one positive charge higher than base.

Advantages

1. Acidity and basicity both are associated with H^+ ions.

2. It is not restricted to bases which contain OH- ions

Limitation

1. Not applicable in non-proton solvents. e.g. BF_3, $POCl_3$, SO_2.

3. Lewis Theory (1923)

Acid: Electron pair acceptor.

Base: Electron pair donor.

When they react they form new co-ordinate compound.

e.g. $\overset{..}{N}H_3 + BF_3 \rightleftharpoons H_3N : BF_3$

              Base Acid

Advantages

1. Not restricted to compounds proton containing proton and hydroxyl ions.

2. Not restricted to particular category of solvent.

Limitations

1. Electronic configuration and valency of substance must be known.

2. Restricted to only electron exchange.

4. Usanovich Theory (1934)

Acid: Chemical species which react with base by giving cations or accepting anions/electrons.

Base: Chemical species which react with acid by giving anions/electrons or accepting cations.

e.g. $Fe^{2+} \rightleftharpoons Fe^{3+} + e^-$

                                        Base   Acid

Advantages

1. Not limited to proton or electron exchange.

2. Able to explain behaviour of oxidizing, reducing agents.

5. Lux-Flood Concept (1929 and 1947)

Acid: Oxide ion acceptor.

Base: Oxide ion donor.

$$MgO + SiO_2 \rightarrow MgSiO_3$$

                Base   Acid   Salt

$$CaO + SO_3 \rightarrow CaSO_4$$

                Base   Acid   Salt

Limitation

1. Restricted to exchange of only oxide ion.

6. Solvent Theory [Franklin 1905]

Acid: Substance which yields cation of a solvent.

Base: Substance which yields anion of the solvent.

e.g. $HCl + H_2O \rightarrow H_3O^+ + Cl^-$

                Acid Solvent   Cation

                $NH_3 + H_2O \rightarrow NH_4^+ + OH^-$

                Base Solvent   Anion

3.2 ACID BASE EQUILIBRIA IN WATER

* Considering acid as 'HA' and base as 'A⁻' its equilibrium in water can be expressed as

$$HA \;+\; H_2O \; \overset{K_a}{\rightleftharpoons} \; H_3O^+ \;+\; A^- \qquad \text{... (1)}$$

Acid   Water   Hydronium ion   conjugate base

$$A^- \;+\; H_2O \; \overset{K_a}{\rightleftharpoons} \; HA \;+\; OH^- \qquad \text{... (2)}$$

Base   Water   Conjugate   Hydroxyl

acid   ion

Water acts as both acid and base and is capable of reacting with base and acid respectively.

Strengths of acid and base are indicated by their dissociation constants K_a and K_b respectively.

Applying law of mass action to equation (1) and (2), we get,

$$K_a \;=\; \frac{[H_3O]^+ + [A^-]}{[HA]} \qquad \text{... (3)}$$

$$K_b \;=\; \frac{[HA]\,[OH^-]}{[A]} \qquad \text{... (4)}$$

Similarly, for water,

$$H_2O \; \overset{K_w}{\rightleftharpoons} \; H^+ + OH^-$$

or

$$H_2O + H_2O \; \overset{K_w}{\rightleftharpoons} \; H_3O^+ + OH^-$$

Hence,

$$K_w = [H^+]\,[OH^-] \text{ or } K_w = [H_3O^+]\,[OH^-] \qquad \text{... (5)}$$

In all cases role of water as a solvent is considered as constant and not included in calculation of dissociation constants.

Multiplying equations (3) and (4),

$$K_a \cdot K_b \;=\; \frac{[H_3O^+]\,[A^-]}{[HA]} \times \frac{[HA]\,[OH^-]}{[A^-]}$$

Cancelling similar species, we get,

$$K_a \cdot K_b \;=\; [H_3O^+]\,[OH^-]$$

As per equation (5),

$$K_a\, K_b \;=\; K_w \qquad \text{... (6)}$$

K_w is dissociation constant of water and is also known as ionic product of water.

3.3 THE pH SCALE

Measurement of pH, i.e. acidity or basicity of a solution is crucial in a number of experiments. pH is negative logarithm of hydrogen ion concentration. A low pH value indicates high concentration of H^+ ions while high pH means low concentration of H^+ ions. Hence pH and H^+ ion are inversely related to each other.

pH scale was invented by Soren Peder Pauritz Sorenson. The scale was known as the Sorenson Scale until 1924 and after that it was renamed.

pH scale ranges from 0 to 14 with the number 7 representing neutral. Neutral means it is neither acidic or basic. If the pH is less than 7, it is acidic. If it is higher than 7, it is basic.

The pH scale is logarithmic and as a result each whole pH value below 7 is ten times more acidic than the next higher value. e.g. pH 4 is ten times more acidic than pH 5 and 100 times more acidic than pH 6. Similar is the case with basicity for pH values above 7.

$$pH = -\log [H^+]$$

Square brackets around H^+ mean molar concentration of H^+ ions.

pH is dimensionless quantity. It has no units.

More appropriate definition of pH as per IUPAC (International Union of Pure and Applied Chemistry) is

$$pH = -\log [a(H^+)] = -\log (m_H \gamma_H / m^\circ)$$

$$m_H = \text{Molality}$$

$$m^\circ = \text{Standard molality}$$

$$\gamma = \text{Molal activity coefficient}$$

$a(H^+)$ is activity of hydrogen ion.

Strong acids (HA), dissociate completely in water and they do not exist as acid in the form of HA.

$$HA + H_2O \rightleftharpoons H_3O^+ + A^-$$

The only proton donor and strongest acid that can exist in aqueous solution is H_3O^+ i.e. hydronium ion. Hence, sometimes pH is called as negative log of concentration of hydronium ion instead of hydrogen ion.

Thus pH scale conveniently expresses $[H^+]$ values by compressing a wide range of $[H^+]$ values into a small measurable range of numbers.

3.4 DISTRIBUTION OF ACID BASE SPECIES WITH pH

- Distribution of acids and bases largely depends on their strength. This strength is relatively expressed as strong or weak.

- Stronger acids and bases dissociate completely when dissolved in a suitable solvent.

- Weaker acids and bases poorly dissociate upon dissolution in their solvents.

- Extent of dissociation can be easily studied by dissociation constants for acids (K_a), bases (K_b) and water (K_w).

- Values of most dissociation constants are very small, hence they are conveniently expressed as pK values.

$$pK_a = -\log K_a$$
$$pK_b = -\log K_b$$
$$pK_w = -\log K_w$$

As per equation number (6),

$$K_w = K_a K_b$$
$$pK_w = pK_a + pK_b$$

pK_w at 25°C is 14, thus,

$$pK_a + pK_b = 14$$

- Strength of the acids and bases easily reflects in values of pK_a. For acids, lower pKa values represent strong acids and for bases also lower pK_b values are characteristic of stronger bases.

  On the contrary, weak acids have higher pK_a values and weak bases have higher pK_b values.

3.4.1 Strong Acids and Bases

Stronger acids like HCl, HClO$_4$, H$_2$SO$_4$, HNO$_3$ and stronger bases like NaOH, KOH, LiOH, Ca(OH)$_2$ dissociate completely in aqueous solvent and their ionisation does not depend on pH.

Table 3.1: pK values of common acids and bases in aqueous solution at 25°C

Acid	pK$_a$	Base	pK$_b$
HClO$_4$	−7	NaOH	0.2
HCl	−3	KOH	0.5
H$_2$SO$_4$	−3	LiOH	−0.36
HNO$_3$	−1	Ca(OH)$_2$	2.43

For calculating pH of strong acid, negative log of $[H^+]$ is taken.

e.g. 0.0154 in HCl will have pH 1.81.

$$pH = -\log[0.0154]$$

For bases, pH can be found as follows.

e.g. pH of 0.01 N KOH is 12.

As it is 0.01 N,

$$[OH^-] = 0.01$$
$$p[OH] = -\log \text{ of } 0.01$$
$$pOH = 2$$
$$pH + pOH = 14$$
$$pH = 14 - pOH$$
$$pH = 12$$

3.4.2 Weak Acids and Bases

Weak acids like acetic acid, boric acid, carbonic acid, HCN and weak bases like ammonia, aniline, pyridine, hydrazine dissociate partially and their ionisation is strongly influenced by the pH of the solution.

Generally acids ionise at alkaline pH and remain unionised at acidic pH. While bases are unionised at alkaline pH and are ionised at acidic pH.

Table 3.2: pK values of weak acids and bases in aqueous solution at 25°

Acid	pK$_a$	Base	pK$_b$
Acetic acid	4.76	Ammonia	4.74
Boric acid	9.24	Pyridine	8.77
Carbonic acid	6.37	Aniline	9.42
Hydrocyanic acid	9.21	Hydrazine	5.82

For calculating pH of solutions of weak acids and bases certain steps have to be followed.

1. e.g. pH of 0.01 M acetic acid is 3.39.

$$pH = -\log[H^+]$$

For weak acids $[H^+] = \sqrt{K_a C}$

So, $pH = -\log \sqrt{K_a C}$

1. As $pK_a = -\log K_a$ $K_a = $ Antilog pK_a

    pK_a of acetic acid is 4.76 $K_a = -$ Antilog $4.76 = 1.75 \times 10^{-5}$

2. $K_a \cdot C = 1.75 \times 10^{-5} \times 0.01 = 1.75 \times 10^{-7}$

3. $\sqrt{K_a C} = \sqrt{1.75 \times 10^{-9}} = 4.18 \times 10^{-4}$

4. $-\log \sqrt{K_a C} = -\log 4.18 \times 10^{-4} = 3.39$.

2. pH of weak base 0.025 M potassium benzoate (pK_b = 9.80) is 8.30.

(i) For bases $[OH] = \sqrt{K_b C}$

$$pH = 14 - pOH$$

$$pOH = -\log [OH^-]$$

Hence, as $pK_b = 9.80$

$$K_b = -\text{Antilog } 9.80$$

$$= 1.60 \times 10^{-10}$$

(ii) $\sqrt{K_b C} = \sqrt{1.60 \times 10^{-10} \times 0.025}$

$$= 2 \times 10^{-6}$$

(iii) $pOH = -\log \sqrt{K_b C}$

$$= -\log 2 \times 10^{-6}$$

$$= 5.70$$

(iv) $pH = 14 - pOH$

$$= 14 - 5.70$$

$$= 8.30$$

3.4.3 Salts of Weak Acids and Bases

- Salt is a combination of an anion and cation. In solid form ions are held together by the difference in their charge. Solid salts usually make crystals, sometimes including specific molar amounts of water called water of hydration.

- If a salt dissolves in water solution, it dissociates into the anions and cations which make up that salt.

- Salts of weak acids produce basic solutions. Salts of weak bases produces acid solutions.

e.g. NH_4OH + $HCl \rightarrow NH_4Cl + H_2O$

    Weak base Strong   Acidic   Water
              acid   salt

    $2NaOH + H_2CO_3 \rightarrow Na_2CO_3 + 2H_2O$

    Strong   Weak   Basic   Water
    base   base   salt

This is due to the fact that conjugate acids of weak bases are strong and they hydrolyse at pH less than 7.

$$HNO_3 + NH_3 \xrightarrow{\text{Formation}} NH_4NO_3 \xrightarrow{\text{dissociation}} NH_4^+ + NO_3^- + H_2O$$

Strong   Weak   Salt

acid   base $\xrightarrow{\text{Hydrolysis}} H_3O^+ + NH_3$

Strong Weak
acid   base

Similarly, conjugate bases of weak acids are strong and hydrolyse at pH greater than 7.

$$NaOH + HF \xrightarrow{\text{Formation}} H_2O + NaF \xrightarrow{\text{Dissociation}} Na^+ + F^- + H_2O$$

Strong base   weak acid   salt

$\xrightarrow{\text{Hydrolysis}} HF + OH^-$

Weak acid   Strong base

3.4.4 Polyprotic Acids and their Salts

- Polyprotic acids contain more than one mole ionisable hydrogen ions per mole of acids. So per molecule, they ionise to give more than one H^+ ion. They ionise in different stages, loosing one H^+ ion at a time.

- Thus, they have multiple protons and contain two or more acidic hydrogens. They have multiple pK_a values.

  Monoprotic acids - HCN, HNO_2 (Nitrous acid), HNO_3 (Nitric acid)

  Polyprotic acids
  - Diprotic - H_2SO_4 (Sulphuric acid), $H_2C_2O_4$ (Oxalic acid), H_2CO_3 (Carbonic acid)
  - Triprotic - H_3PO_4(Phosphoric acid), H_3BO_3(Boric acid)

$$H_3PO_4 + H_2O \rightleftharpoons H_3O^+ + H_2PO_4^- \qquad\qquad K_{a_1} = 7.1 \times 10^{-3}$$

$$H_2PO_4^- + H_2O \rightleftharpoons H_3O^+ + HPO_4^{2-} \qquad\qquad K_{a_2} = 6.2 \times 10^{-8}$$

$$HPO_4^{2-} + H_2O \rightleftharpoons H_3O^+ + PO_4^{3-} \qquad\qquad K_{a_3} = 4.4 \times 10^{-13}$$

$$K_{a_1} > K_{a_2} > K_{a_3}$$

- Salts of polyprotic acids can be either acidic [HSO_4Na] or basic (NH_2HCO_3) because at equilibrium many species will be present in the solution with different pK values. Solution will reflect behaviour as per average pK values.

e.g.

NaH$_2$PO$_4$ K_{a_1} = 7.5×10^{-3} pK_{a_1} = 2.12 Avg. pK = 4.67 acidic pH

                   K_{a_2} = 6.2×10^{-8} pK_{a_2} = 7.21

NaHPO$_4$ K_{a_2} = 6.2×10^{-13} pK_{a_3} = 7.21   Avg. = 9.83 basic pH

                   K_{a_3} = 4.4×10^{-13} pK_{a_3} = 12.44

NaHCO$_3$ K_{a_1} = 4.5×10^{-7} pK_{a_1} = 6.35   Avg = 8.34 basic pH

                   K_{a_2} = 4.7×10^{-11} pK_{a_2} = 10.33

3.5 BUFFER SOLUTIONS

Buffers: Solutions which resist change in pH when small amount of acid or base is added to them or when they are diluted are known as buffers.

Buffers are usually prepared as a mixture of weak acid and its conjugate base or weak base and its conjugate acid at predetermined concentration.

e.g.

$HA \rightleftharpoons H^+ + A^-$ Acid Conjugate base $K_a = \dfrac{[H^+][A^-]}{[HA]}$ $[H^+] = K_a \dfrac{[HA]}{[A^-]}$	$CH_3COOH \rightleftharpoons H^+ + CH_3COO^-$ Acid Conjugate base $K_a = \dfrac{[H^+][CH_3COO^-]}{[CH_3COOH]}$ $[H^+] = K_a \dfrac{[CH_3COOH]}{[CH_3COO^-]}$
Taking negative log on both sides.	
$pH = pK_a + \log \dfrac{[A^-]}{[HA]}$ $pK_a = pH - \log \dfrac{[A^-]}{[HA]}$	or $pH = pK_a + \log \dfrac{[CH_3COO^-]}{[CH_3COOH]}$ $pK_a = pH - \log \dfrac{[CH_3COO^-]}{[CH_3COO^-]}$

This is called as Henderson Hasselbalch equation.

How buffer resists change in pH?

According to Henderson Hasselbalch equation, pH of a solution is related to pK$_a$ and log of ratio of concentration of conjugate base and acid. So a buffer made up of an acid and its conjugate base has a specific pH.

It has some specific pH, which does not change on dilution or addition of acid/base.

1. On Dilution

When a buffer solution is diluted,

$$pH = pK_a + \log \frac{[A^-]}{[HA]}$$

pH is dependent on pK_a and ratio of $\log \dfrac{[A^-]}{[HA]}$

pK_a is constant and does not change on dilution.

Even, on dilution ratio of $[A^-]$ and $[HA]$ does not change or change very slightly, so there is no net change in concentration and pH.

2. Upon addition of a strong acid or a strong base

$$HA + A^- \quad + \quad HCl \rightarrow 2HA + Cl^-$$

Buffer   Strong

         acid

So strong acid reacts with conjugate base to form more amount of acid.

If strong base is added.

$$HA + A^- \quad + \quad NaOH \rightarrow H_2O + 2A^- + Na^+$$

Buffer   Strong

         base

So addition of strong base leads to reaction with HA to form more amount of conjugate base.

This may lead to change in ratio of $[A^-]/[HA]$ and ultimately pH.

But this will not happen because, according to Le Chatelier principle - added H^+/OH^- will combine with A^- or HA to form HA or A^- if and only if there is excess of A^- or HA.

Addition of small amount of strong acid or base changes pH very slightly.

e.g. Buffer : Acetic acid + Sodium acetate

      0.1 M (50 ml)   0.1 M (50 ml)

$$pH = pK_a + \log \frac{[\text{Sodium acetate}]}{[\text{Acetic acid}]}$$

As both are 0.1 M and 50 ml, ratio is 1 and log of 1 is zero.

$$pH = pK_a + 0$$

$$pH = 4.76 \text{ [Equal to } pK_a \text{ of acetic acid i.e. 4.76]}$$

Now if 1 ml of 0.1 N NaOH is added.

$$CH_3COOH + CH_3COONa + NaOH \rightarrow 2CH_3COONa + H_2O$$

     Buffer   Strong base

                Initial   Reacted

$$[\text{Acetic acid}] = 100\,(0.1) - 1\,(0.1)$$

$$= 10 - 0.1 = 9.9$$

$$\text{Initial} \qquad \text{Formed}$$

$$[\text{Sodium acetate}] = 100\,(0.1) + 1\,(0.1)$$

$$= 10 + 0.1 = 10.1$$

So, $\qquad$ new pH $= \text{pK}_a + \log \dfrac{10.1}{9.9}$

$$= \text{pK}_a + \log 1.02 \qquad (\text{Exact log of 1.02 is 0.0086})$$

$$= 4.76 + 0.01$$

$$= 4.77$$

So pH shifts from 4.76 to 4.77 which is very negligible, hence addition of strong acid or base in small amount does not change the pH of buffer very significantly.

Buffer capacity/Buffer index/Buffer intensity (β)

$$\beta = \frac{dB}{dpH}$$

$$dB = \beta \times dpH$$

Buffer index/capacity/intensity is magnitude of buffer strength i.e. its ability to resist change in pH. Higher the value of 'β', higher is the ability to resist change in pH.

dB is the concentration of strong base or acid to be added and dpH is the change in pH.

So 'β' is nothing but amount of strong base/acid required to be added to change pH by 1 amount.

e.g. if β = 0.05 of any buffer it means 0.05 mole of strong base or strong acid to be added and pH of buffer will change by 1 unit.

So if any buffer has high 'β' value it means more amount of base/acid should be added to change its pH by 1.

'β' is maximum when there is equal concentration of acid and its salt.

Calculation of 'β' involves concentration of both acid and its conjugate base.

$$\beta = \frac{C_{HA}C_{A^-}}{C_{HA} + C_{A^-}}$$

where, $\qquad$ C = Concentration

e.g. If 0.1 M acetic acid and 0.1 M sodium acetate are used to prepare buffer,

$$\beta = \frac{0.1 \times 0.1}{0.1 + 0.1} = \frac{0.01}{0.2} = 0.05$$

Now, if 0.2 M acetic acid and 0.2 M sodium acetate are used to prepare buffer,

$$\beta = \frac{0.2 \times 0.2}{0.2 + 0.2} = \frac{0.04}{0.4} = 0.1$$

If both acetic acid and sodium acetate are 1M.

$$\beta = 0.5$$

Buffer capacity is higher than first two cases.

Acceptable buffer capacity is $pK_a \pm 1$.

'β' is maximum when $pH = pK_a$

Problems

1. **Calculate pH of a mixture of 10 ml 0.1 M acetic acid and 20 ml 0.1 M sodium acetate [pK_a = 4.76].**

$$pH = pK_a + \log \frac{[A^-]}{[HA]}$$

Here,   HA = Acetic acid 0.1 M, 10 ml $[HA] = 0.1 \times 10$

A$^-$ = Sodium acetate 0.1 M, 20 ml $[A^-] = 0.1 \times 20$

$$pH = 4.76 + \log \frac{[01. \times 20]}{[0.1 \times 10]} = pH = 4.76 + \log 2$$

log of 2 is 0.3

$$pH = 4.76 + 0.3$$
$$= 5.06$$

2. **Calculate pH of 10 ml acetate buffer containing equal volume of 0.2 M acetic acid and 0.2 M acetate after addition of 1 ml 0.1 M HCl.**

$$\text{Initial pH} = pK_a + \log \frac{[A^-]}{[HA]}$$

$$= 4.76 + \log \frac{5 \text{ ml} \times 0.2/10}{5 \text{ ml} \times 0.2/10}$$

$$= 4.76 + \log 1$$
$$= 4.76 + 0$$
$$= 4.76$$

When 0.1 M 1 ml HCl is added.

$$CH_3COOH + CH_3COO^- + HCl \rightarrow 2CH_3COOH + Cl^-$$

            Buffer   added acid

Concentration of CH_3COOH increases 5 (0.2) + 1 (0.1) = 1.1

Concentration of CH_3COO^- decreases 5 (0.2) − 1 (0.1) = 0.9

$$pH = 4.76 \log \frac{0.9}{1.1}$$

$$pH = 4.76 \log 0.81$$
$$pH = 4.76 - 0.09$$
$$= 4.66$$

Calculation of pH of mixtures

1. Mixture of strong acid and base

e.g. Calculate pH of solution containing 50 ml of 0.1 M HCl and 8 ml of 0.5 M NaOH.

$$pH = -\log [H^+]$$

As this is mixture of acid and base, we need to consider concentration of H^+ ion as initially present and that reacted.

Initial present $[H^+]$ = 50 (0.1) = 5 m mole

Reacted, because of NaOH = 8 (0.5) = 4 m mole

So total (H^+) present = 5 - 4 = 1 m mole in total 58 ml.

$$[H^+] = 1/58$$

$$= 0.0172$$

$$pH = -\log [H^+]$$

$$pH = -\log 0.0172$$

$$= -\log 1.72 \times 10^{-2}$$

$$= 2 - \log 1.72$$

$$= 2 - 0.02355$$

$$pH = 1.76$$

2. Mixture of weak acid and strong base

Calculate pH of solution containing 50 ml of 0.1 M CH₃COOH and 10 ml of 0.1 M NaOH.

$$pK_a = 4.76$$

Normally, $[H^+] = \sqrt{K_a C}$

For mixtures

$$pH = pK_a + \log \frac{[A^-]}{[HA]}$$

Here,   HA = CH_3COOH [50 ml, 0.1 M]

Base = NaOH [10 ml, 0.1 m]

$$HA + B \rightleftharpoons A^- + H^+$$

$$HA + B \rightleftharpoons CH_3COONa + H_2O$$

$[A^-]$ = Amount of CH_3COOH reacted

$$= \frac{Concentration}{Volume} = \frac{10\ (0.1)}{50 + 10} = \frac{1}{60}$$

$$[HA] = \text{Amount of acid remaining}$$
$$= \frac{\text{Concentration}}{\text{Volume}} = \frac{50\,(0.1) - 10\,(0.1)}{50 + 60} = \frac{4}{60}$$
$$pH = 4.76 + \log\frac{1/60}{4/60}$$
$$= 4.76 + \log\frac{1}{4}$$
$$= 4.76 + \log 0.25$$
$$= 4.76 - 0.6$$
$$= 4.16$$

3.6 STANDARD SOLUTIONS

Solutions whose strength is accurately known are called as standard solutions. If not known, it is determined by their titration against 1° standard; this process is known as standardisation. Therefore, standardisation is a process of analysing accurately the strength of a solution by titrating it with a substance whose purity is known. In short, standardisation is finding out the exact molarity/normality of solution.

Primary standard: A substance of known purity which can be weighed and dissolved in a solution to give solution of known strength is known as primary standard e.g. Potassium hydrogen phthalate, oxalic acid, sodium carbonate.

Need of standardisation of titrants

*   Strong acids and bases are not commercially available in forms of accurately known concentration, so they are prepared approximately to the desired concentration and then standardised.

*   Many strong acids and bases are not sufficiently soluble in water. So when they are diluted, strength cannot be predicted.

*   Many solutions once prepared, undergo decrease in strength upon storage [because of CO_2] hence need to be standardised before use.

    So, titrants upon standardisation are called as standard solutions.

How standard solutions are prepared

Molar solutions: If a substance is solid, molecular weight is determined [e.g. NaOH → 40] and one gram equivalent means it is converted in grams [NaOH → 40 gm] and dissolved in 1000 ml solvent.

So 40 gm NaOH in 1000 ml water is 1M NaOH solution.

Normal solutions: Here equivalent weight is taken in grams and dissolved in 1000 ml solvent.

e.g. 1) 40 gm NaOH in 1000 ml water is 1N NaOH

$$\text{equivalent weight for acid base titration} = \frac{\text{Molecular weight}}{H^+ \text{ given or taken}}$$

For NaOH molecular weight = Equivalent weight

∴   1M = 1N

2)   For Preparation of 1M HCl

Now, molecular weight of HCl = 36.5.

But 36.5 g in 1000 ml will not yield 1M solution.

This is because

a.   HCl is not a solid to be weighed.

b.   Solution available commercially is of strength 36% v/v.

So, these two problems are solved one by one. We need 36.5 gm of HCl to dissolve in 1000 ml water.

a.   Density of HCl is 1.18.

$$D = \frac{M}{V}$$

So $V = \frac{M}{D}$

Mass we need is 36.5.   D = 1.18

$$\text{Volume which contains 36.5 g of acid} = \frac{36.5}{1.18}$$

$$= 30.93 \text{ ml}$$

So we can take 30.93 ml of HCl in 1000 ml of water.

b.   Now commercially available HCl solutions are of 36% v/v.

Means they have 36 ml HCl in 100 ml water.

We need only 30.93 ml HCl

So, 100 ml contains 36 ml HCl

x ml will contain 30.93 HCl

$$x = \frac{100 \times 30.93}{36}$$

$$x = 85.9 \text{ ml}$$

So we need to take 85 ml of concentrated HCl and dissolve it in 1000 ml water to give 1M HCl. Similarly 8.5 ml conc. HCl in 1000 ml water → 0.1 M HCl.

[85.9 ml need not be taken accurately because solution is standardised afterwards using sodium carbonate to determine actual molarity].

For HCl,   1M = 1N

Therefore,Molecular weight = Equivalent weight

3)   To prepare 1M H_2SO_4 solution,

Molecular weight of H_2SO_4 = 98 gm

So 98 gm is to be dissolved in 1000 ml

a.   But, H_2SO_4 is liquid with D = 1.83

So $V = \dfrac{M}{D} = \dfrac{98}{1.83} = 53.55$ ml

So 53.55 ml in 1000 ml

b.   Commercially available concentrated H_2SO_4 is 98% v/v.

So 100 ml solution contains 98 ml of H_2SO_4

x ml has 53.55 ml of H_2SO_4

∴   x = 54 ml

So 54 ml concentrated H_2SO_4 in 1000 ml → 1M H_2SO_4

As molecular weight = 2 × Equivalent weight

1M = 2N

So 1N H_2SO_4 = 27 ml concentrated H_2SO_4 in 1000 ml.

Neutralisation Titration

In these types of titrations, acids and bases [one is taken as titrant, other as analyte] are titrated together and when they react, because of their opposite nature, neutralisation of each other's character takes place. They form salt and water when both react completely i.e. when analyte has consumed titrant equal to its strength. Indicators show colour change mainly because of change in pH at the end point.

3.7 TITRATION CURVES

During neutralisation titration, pH of analyte solution continuously changes as titrant is added. e.g. acid vs. base titration.

Initial pH - acidic [because of acid]

At end point, pH - Neutral [because of complete reaction of acid and base]

After end point, pH - Alkaline [because of excess of base]

So, pH changes during titration. If this pH is measured and plotted against the volume of titrant (v) added, it generates a sigmoidal plot known as neutralisation curve.

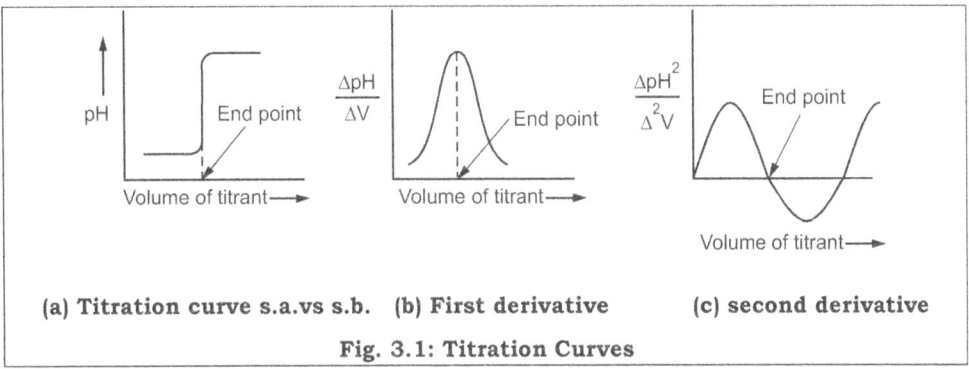

(a) Titration curve s.a.vs s.b. **(b) First derivative**   **(c) second derivative**

Fig. 3.1: Titration Curves

If analyte is basic and strong acid is titrant.

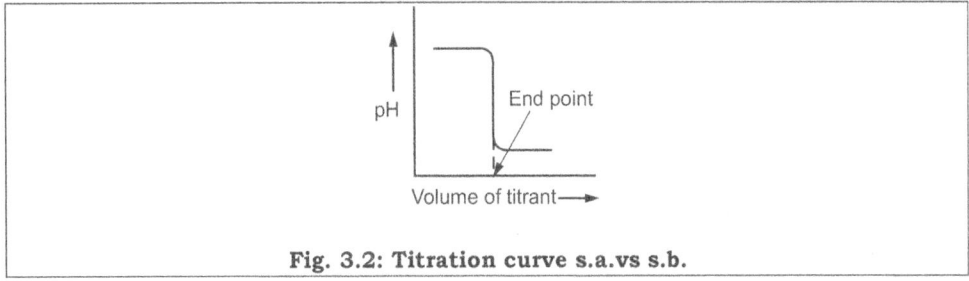

Fig. 3.2: Titration curve s.a.vs s.b.

Shape of normal curve is sigmoidal and becomes steep depending on type of titration (Fig. 3.2) and strength of acid (Fig. 3.3).

e.g.

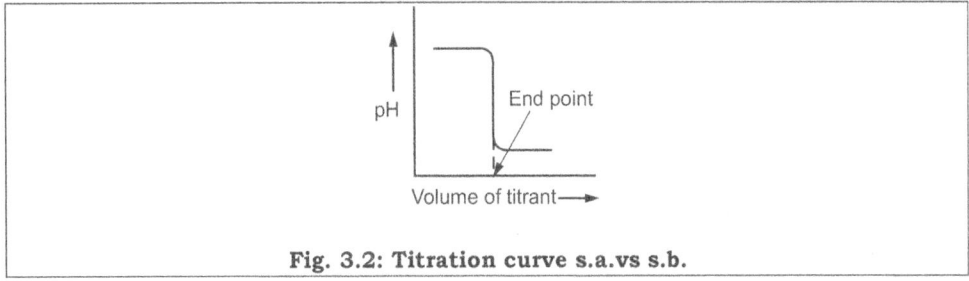

Fig. 3.3: Titration curve strong acid vs strong base at different strengths

1. **Strong acid vs. Strong base** (100ml, 1N HCl vs. 1N NaOH)

$$H^+ + Cl^- + Na^+ + OH^- \rightarrow H_2O + Na^+Cl^-$$

pH before titration is because of HCl.

$$[H^+] = 1N$$
$$pH = -\log [H^+] = -\log 1$$
$$pH = 0$$

After addition of 1ml NaOH $\rightarrow [H^+] = \dfrac{100\,(1) - 1\,(1)}{100 + 1}$

$$= \dfrac{99}{101} = 0.98$$

$$[H^+] = 0.98$$

$$pH = 0.008$$

After addition of ml of NaOH	Concentration of [H⁺]	pH
50 ml	3.33×10^{-1}	0.33
90 ml	5.27×10^{-2}	1.3
99.9 ml	5.01×10^{-4}	3.3
100 ml	-	7
101 ml	$1/2015 \times 10^3$	11.7

So, pH rises gradually initially $[0 \rightarrow 0.33 \rightarrow 1.3 \rightarrow 3]$ but it rises suddenly [from 3.3 to 7] at the end point, after that again change in pH occurs slowly.

2. **Titration of weak acid vs. Strong base**

e.g. 100 ml 0.1 M CH_3COOH vs. 0.1 M NaOH.

$CH_3COOH + Na^+ + OH^- \rightarrow H_2O + Na^+ + CH_3COO^-$

(a) Initial pH

Acetic acid is a weak acid.

Initial pH depends on

$$[H^+] = \sqrt{k_a C} = \sqrt{1.82 \times 10^{-6}} = 1.35 \times 10^{-3}$$

$$pH = 2.87$$

After 50 ml addition of alkali

$$pH = pK_a + \log \dfrac{[A^-]}{[HA]} = pK_a + \log \dfrac{3.33 \times 10^{-2}}{3.33 \times 10^{-2}} = 4.76$$

After 99.9 ml addition of NaOH, pH = 7.7.

After 100 ml addition of NaOH, pH = 8.7.

After 101 ml addition of NaOH, pH = 10.7.

So at end point pH rises from 7.7 to 8.7, range is quite small. After end point pH is 10.7.

So indicator must be chosen which has transition interval from pH 7.7 to 10. e.g. Phenolphthalein.

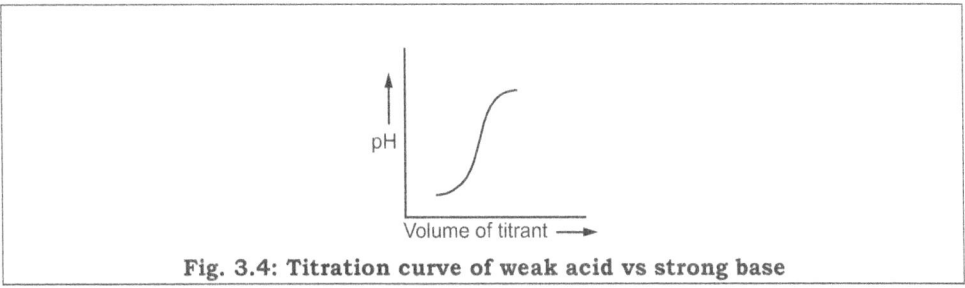

Fig. 3.4: Titration curve of weak acid vs strong base

pH at equivalence point.

$$= \sqrt{\frac{k_w}{k_a} \cdot C_A} = 8.72$$

Point of Titration	Equation to calculate pH
1. Initial stage	$H^+ = \sqrt{k_aC}$
B.R. = 0 ml	$pH = -\log \sqrt{k_aC}$
2. Before end point	$pH = pK_a + \log \dfrac{C_{A^-}}{C_{HA}}$
3. At equivalence point	$pH = \sqrt{\dfrac{k_w}{k_a} \cdot C_{A^-}}$
4. After equivalence point	$pH = pK_w - \log [OH^-]$ (excess titrant)

3. Titration of weak base vs. Strong acid

e.g. $NH_3 + H^+ + Cl \rightarrow NH_4^+ + Cl^-$

As base is analyte, initial pH is high which decreases gradually during titration and suddenly at end point. Buffer region exists before and after equivalence point.

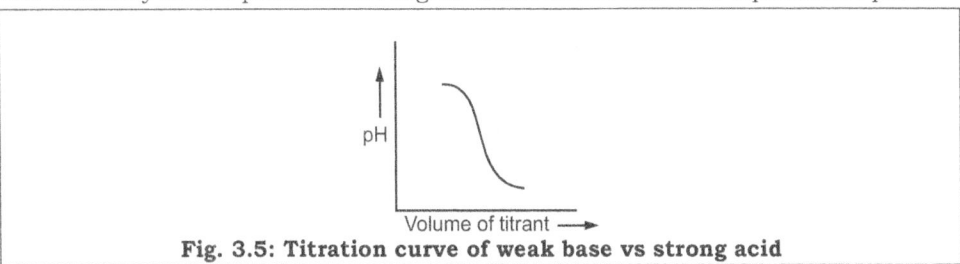

Fig. 3.5: Titration curve of weak base vs strong acid

pH at equivalence point $= \sqrt{\dfrac{k_w}{k_b} C \cdot BH^+}$

Point of Titration	Equation to calculate pH
1. Initial stage	$pH = pK_w - \log [OH^-]$ $[OH^-] = \sqrt{kbC}$
2. Before equivalence point	$pH = (pK_w - pK_b) + \log \dfrac{C_B}{C_{BH^+}}$
3. At equivalence point	$pH = \sqrt{\dfrac{k_w}{k_b} C_{BH^+}}$
4. After equivalence point	$pH = -\log [H^+]$ (excess titrant)

4. Weak acid vs. Weak bases

Such titrations are avoided because pH change at equivalence point is so narrow, indicators are not available.

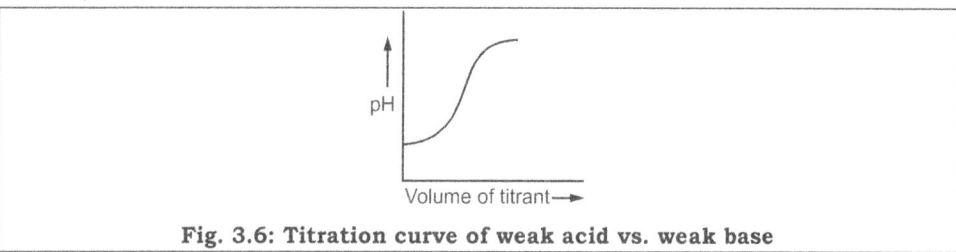

Fig. 3.6: Titration curve of weak acid vs. weak base

5. Titrations of polyfunctional acids and bases

- As polybasic acids contain multiple protons, when they are titrated against strong bases, there are multiple equivalence points.

- They loose protons in stepwise manner and show two buffer regions. Titration curves are sigmoidal in shape as that of monoprotic acids and bases.

e.g. $H_2SO_4 \rightarrow H^+ + HSO_4^-$

$HSO_4^- \rightarrow H^+ + SO_4^-$

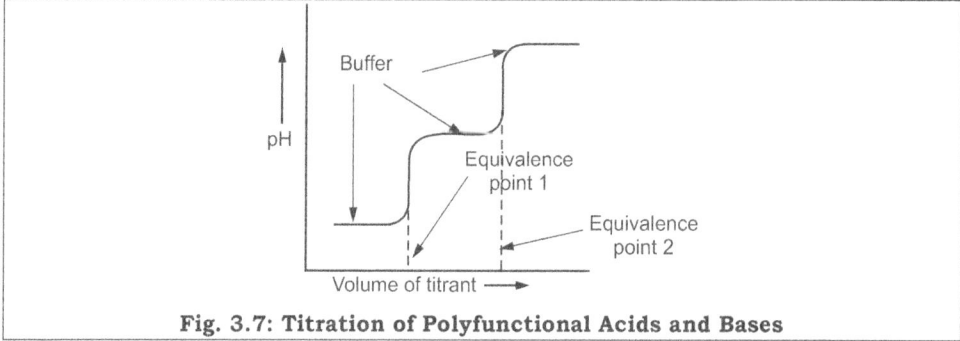

Fig. 3.7: Titration of Polyfunctional Acids and Bases

1. pH prior to titration will be same as that of strong or weak acid.
$$[H^+] = \sqrt{K_a C}$$

2. pH in first buffer region prior to equivalence point.
$$[H^+] = \frac{K_{a_1} [H_2A]}{[HA^-]}$$

3. pH at equivalence point
$$[H^+] = \sqrt{K_{a_1} K_{a_2}}$$

4. pH at second buffer region
$$[H^+] = \frac{K_{a_2} [HA^-]}{[A^{2-}]}$$

5. pH at second equivalence point
$$[OH^-] = \sqrt{C_b \frac{K_w}{K_{a_2}}}$$

6. pH after second equivalence point
$$[OH] = \text{Moles of } [OH^-] - \text{Moles of } [H_3O^+]$$

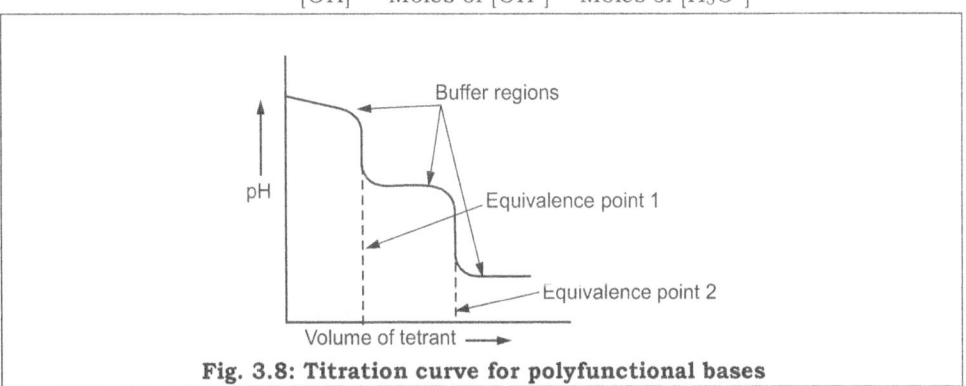

Fig. 3.8: Titration curve for polyfunctional bases

Here also two equivalence points will appear and pH at every stage can be calculated.

3.8 THEORIES OF ACID BASE INDICATORS

Acid base indicators/neutralisation indicators are chosen such that they show colour change at end point of titration.

There are two theories which demonstrate mechanism of action of indicator.

1. Ostwald Theory

This theory relies on the fact that indicator is capable of ionisation and it has two different colours in ionised and unionised form. It is assumed that indicators are very weak organic acids or bases.

$$HIn_A \rightleftharpoons H^+ + In_B^-$$

Unionised	Ionised
colour 1	colour 2

Therefore, observed colour of indicator in solution is dependent on ratio of concentration of both forms ionised and unionised i.e. acidic and basic forms and hence it is directly proportional to pH.

$$KIn_a = \frac{[H^+] \, [In_B^-]}{[HIn_A]}$$

$$\left(\begin{array}{c}\text{Dissociation} \\ \text{constant}\end{array}\right)$$

$$pH = pKIn_a + \log \frac{[In_B]}{[HIn_A]}$$

As colours depend on concentration of H^+ ion and hence pH, when there is gradual change in H^+ ion concentration, there is gradual change in colour of indicator.

In order to detect colour change, ratio of ionised and unionised forms i.e. $[In^-]/[HIn]$ must be at least 0.1 i.e. 1/10. The pH values at which these limits exists are

$$pH = pKIn_a + \log \frac{[In^-]}{[HIn]}$$

For acidic side, $pH = pKIn - 1$

For basic side, $pH = pKIn + 1$

So pH range in which colour change is observed is

$$pH = pKIn \pm 1$$

This is called as transition interval of indicator so indicator should be chosen such that pH at equivalence point falls within the transition interval of the indicator.

Indicator	Colour in acid	Transition interval	Colour
Phenolphthalein	Colourless	8.3-11	Red
Methyl red	Red	4.2-6.3	Yellow
Phenol red	Yellow	6.8-8.4	Red

2. Resonance theory

It is based on assumption that indicators are organic compounds and colour of indicator depends on their organic structure. As structure changes in acidic and basic pH [means with different pH], it leads to colour change.

Ultimately, structure decides electronic distribution within compound and hence a different structure leads to different electronic framework. Colour of any compound depends mostly on absorption of visible light [made up of 7 colours] and electrons are responsible for this absorption. As electronic framework changes, colour of compound also changes.So indicators must be chosen such that they have different structures before and after equivalence point. This is quite possible with respect to different pH. As solution has different pH before and after equivalence point, indicator has different structure. Generally ionic forms have greater possibilities of resonance and they have intense colours. e.g. Phenolphthalein.

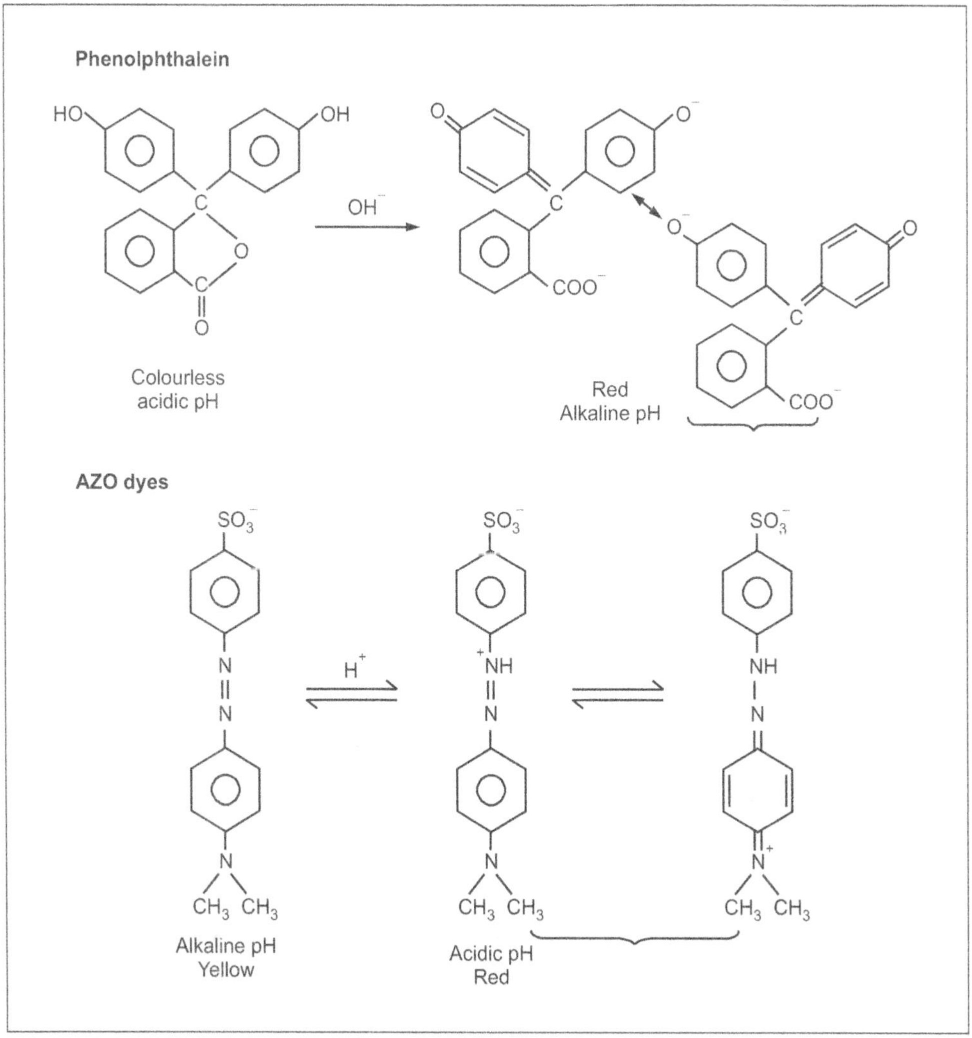
Phenolphthalein
HO
OH
C
O
C
O
OH⁻
O
O⁻
C
COO⁻
O⁻
O
C
COO⁻
Colourless
acidic pH
Red
Alkaline pH
AZO dyes
SO3⁻
N
N
N
CH3 CH3
Alkaline pH
Yellow
H⁺
SO3⁻
⁺NH
N
N
CH3 CH3
Acidic pH
Red
SO3⁻
NH
N
N⁺
CH3 CH3

Types of Neutralisation Indicators

1. Simple indicators

They are used alone and are either weak acids or weak bases. They show colour change because of change in pH. They are chosen such that they undergo ionisation or structural change during equivalence point to show colour change.

pH range

e.g.   Phenolphthalein   8.3 – 11

            Methyl Red   4.2 – 6.3

They are selected based on pH at equivalence point. pH should be between transition interval of indicator.

They are added at the beginning of titration and usually a drop is sufficient.

e.g. 1) Phenolphthalein - 5g in 500 mL ethanol + 500 mL water with stirring. Filter if precipitate forms.

2) Methyl Red - 1g free acidic form in 1L of hot water or 1g in 600 mL ethanol and 400 mL water.

2. Mixed indicators

If the pH range is too narrow at the equivalence point, or if suitable indicator is not available [if its transition interval does not match to equivalence point pH], mixture of two or more indicators is used to obtain sharp colour change.

They need to be selected such that their pKIn values are close to each other and overlapping colours are complementary.

e.g. 1) Mixture of Methyl red + Methylene blue [equal parts, 0.1% solution in alcohol].

Colour changes from violet [acidic pH] to green [alkaline pH] over neutral pH of 7 in between.

2) Phenolphthalein [0.1%] and α naphtholphthalein [0.1%]

3 : 1

Show colour change from pale rose to violet at pH 8.9.

3. Universal indicators/Multiple range indicators

They consist of mixture of several indicators to show colour change over extended range of pH. They give approximate determination of pH and are used in colourimetry.

e.g. 0.1 g phenolphthalein + 0.2 g Methyl red + 0.3 g Methyl yellow + 0.4 g bromothymol blue + 0.5 g Thymol blue in 500 ml absolute alcohol, add sufficient NaOH to make solution yellow.

pH	2	4	6	8	10
Colour	Red	Orange	Yellow	Green	Blue

3.9 TITRATION OF AMINO ACIDS

- Amino acids are the molecules which contain both carboxylic acid and amino groups. They are present as Zwitter ions/amphoteric molecules at isoelectric pH thus capable of titrating with acid as well as alkali.

- At acidic pH, protonation of amino group results in cationic form while at alkaline pH, dissociation of carboxylic group results in anionic form.

- So any simple amino acid which does not have any acidic/basic group at 'R' in its fully protonated form (at acidic pH) has two phases [diprotic acid] because of amino and carboxylic acid group both are protonated.

- Upon titration with base like NaOH, it will show titration curve similar to weak polyprotic acid.

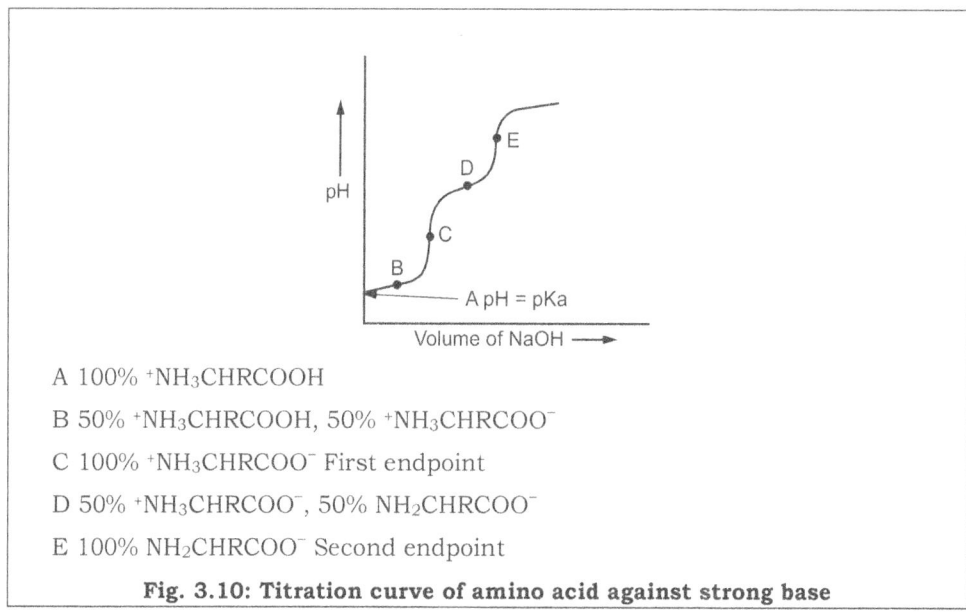

A 100% $^+NH_3CHRCOOH$

B 50% $^+NH_3CHRCOOH$, 50% $^+NH_3CHRCOO^-$

C 100% $^+NH_3CHRCOO^-$ First endpoint

D 50% $^+NH_3CHRCOO^-$, 50% $NH_2CHRCOO^-$

E 100% $NH_2CHRCOO^-$ Second endpoint

Fig. 3.10: Titration curve of amino acid against strong base

- It will be a two stage titration that gives rise to a biphasic graph. If R group contains acidic group stages of reaction and phases in graph will increase.

    $\overset{+}{N}H_3CH(R)COOH \rightarrow NaOH \rightarrow \overset{+}{N}H_3CH(R)COONa + H_2O$

  $\overset{+}{N}H_3CH(R)COOH + NaOH \rightarrow NH_2CH(R)COONa + Na^+ + H_2O$

- There will be two plateau regions. In first plateau region mid point (B) amino acid will be half in the acidic form and half in Zwitter ions form.

- The point of inflection (C) occurs when all of the amino acid is in the Zwitterion form. The pH at which this occurs is isoelectric pH (pI) which marks the end point. At point (D) mid point of second plateau half the amino acid is in Zwitterion form and half is in the basic form.

- Point B gives pK_{acid} [For carboxylic group]

  Point D gives pK_{amine} [For amino group]

  Because pK_a is the pH at which concentration of the protonated and unprotonated forms of a particular ionizable species are equal, according to Henderson-Hasselbalch equation.

  pH $= pK_a + \log \dfrac{[Unprotonated\ form\ (base)]}{[Protonated\ form\ (acid)]}$

- Hence titration curve of amino acids will reflect pK_a, pK_b and isoelectric points.

Have you heard about them?

The concept of pH scale was first introduced by Danish chemist **Soren Peder Lauritz Sorensen** at the Carlsberg Laboratory in the year 1999.

Any chemistry laboratory is incomplete without the pH scale. A pH scale is very important and is required for almost every chemical procedure that is conducted.

Sorensen was born on January 9, 1868, at Havrebjerg, Slagelse, Denmark and belonged to a peasant family. He graduated from the high school in Soro slash in 1886 and entered the University of Copenhagen.

In 1889 Sorensen proved his academic worth by winning a gold medal for an essay on chemical radicals. Soren Peder Lauritz Sorensen was working at the Carlsberg Laboratory and he studied the effect of ion concentration on proteins.

He realized that the concentration of hydrogen ions was particularly important and hence he introduced the pH-scale.

According to him, pH scale was a simple way of expressing it. He introduced the scale using the notation pH and described two new methods for measuring the levels of acids in substances.

The first method was based on electrodes, while the second involved comparing the colours of the samples and a preselected set of indicators.

The scale was later revised to the modern pH in the year 1924 and later it became apparent that electromotive force in cells depends on activity rather than concentration of hydrogen ions.

Lawrence Joseph Henderson (June 3, 1878 - February 10, 1942) was a physiologist, chemist, biologist, philosopher, and sociologist.

He became one of the leading biochemists of the early 20th century. His work contributed to the Henderson-Hasselbalch equation, used to calculate pH as a measure of acidity.

He graduated from Harvard College in 1898 and from Harvard Medical School in 1902, receiving the M.D. (Medical Doctor) degree.

He investigated acid-base regulation in the body. He found that acid-base balance is regulated by buffer systems of the blood in complex coordination with respiration, the lung, red blood cells and with the kidneys.

He wrote the Henderson equation in 1908 to describe the use of carbonic acid as a buffer solution.

Karl Albert Hasselbalch (1st November 1874-19 September 1962) was a physician and chemist. He was a pioneer in the use of pH measurement in medicine (with Christian Bohr, father of Niels Bohr), and he described how the affinity of blood for oxygen was dependent on the concentration of carbon dioxide. In 1916, he converted the equation of Lawrence Joseph Henderson to logarithmic form, which is now known as the Henderson-Hasselbalch equation. Being a medical doctor at the University of Copenhagen he became dedicated in finding the use of pH measurement in blood which eventually led him to become the first person ever to determine the pH of blood.

✱✱✱

4

NON-AQUEOUS ACID BASE TITRATIONS

4.1 Theory

4.2 Types of Solvents in Non-aqueous Titrations

4.3 Indicators

4.4 Preparation and Standardisation of Perchloric Acid, 0.1 M

4.5 Karl Fischer Titration

4.1 THEORY

Acid base titrations performed in solvents other than water [aqueous] are called as non-aqueous titrations. They are widely used for substances which are too weakly basic or acidic to give sharp end point in aqueous system.

In 1912, Folin and Flanders titrated acids in benzene, chloroform and chloroform-ethanol mixtures. In 1927, Conant and Hall reported important investigations about behaviour of bases in glacial acetic acid.

Solvents used in non-aqueous titration must be pure, dry and their hazards must be known.

The reason why water is avoided in non-aqueous titration is that because of its amphoteric nature, water acts as a competetor for weak acids and weak bases for the titrant. Also substances that are not soluble in water, non aqueous solvent are used.

Ideal Properties of Solvents

1. **Self-dissociation:** It is characterised by pKs value, high value means lower dissociation and vice-versa. Dissociation leads to interference in the reaction. Therefore, solvents with high pKs value are preferred. Hence, water is not suitable. e.g. Water - 14, Ethanol - 19.1, Acetonitrile - 26.5.

2. **Dielectric constant:** This is ratio of electrical capacitance of condenser filled with solvent to that of empty condenser. $F = -e^2/Dr^2$.

    High dielectric constant means more separation of charges i.e. more dissociation and interference. Hence, solvent with low dielectric constant are preferred. Water is not such solvent. e.g. Water - 78.5, Ethanol - 24.3, Benzene - 2.27.

3. **Acid base character:** Solvents may possess acidic [proton] or basic [protophilic] character, they are selected as per need of titration.

4.1.1 Non aqueous titrations

1. **Titrations of weak acids.** For titration of weak acids like phenolic compounds, imide solvents used are monoacidic [because bases will enhance acidic character of analyte] or neutral solvents [for mixtures] e.g. ethylene diamine, n-butylamine, pyridine, DMF, methanol, ethanol, acetone.

    *   Methoxides of K, Na form gel in solvents like methanol, benzene/toluene. It can be overcome by adding tetrabutyl ammonium hydroxides.

    *   Appplications: Drugs can be directly analysed from their dosage forms (except those containing stearic acid).

    *   For drug with pK_a 7-11, the endpoint can be determined by potentiometry.

2. **Titrations of weak bases.** For titration of weak bases like amides, caffeine, antipyridine solvents used are either acidic or neutral.

    e.g. Glacial acetic acid, dioxant acetic acid, acetic anhydride [for very weak bases], benzene, chloroform acetonitrile, dioxan.

    *   Mixtures of bases can be determined by use of differentiating solvents.

    *   Substances which are not basic, can be converted to bases and then titrated.

Limitations of Non-aqueous titrations

1. Very few strong titrants are available.

2. All glassware must be dry, free from water.

3. Entry of atmospheric moisture must be avoided during titration.

4.2 TYPES OF SOLVENTS IN NON – AQUEOUS TITRATIONS

Solvents used must be pure, dry and care should be taken while handling them.

1. Aprotic solvents

e.g. Toluene, Chloroform, Carbon tetrachloride.

They are neutral and chemically inert. They have low dielectric constant. They do not donate or accept proton and therefore do not react with either acids or bases. They do not favour ionisation, so they are used for dilution of substances without affecting/reacting with the substance. They are also used to depress solvolysis of neutralisation product and thus for sharpening the end point.

2. Protophilic solvents

e.g. Ether, pyridine, liq. ammonia, acetic anhydride, amines, ketones.

They are basic and have affinity towards protons, so they react with acids.

$$\text{HA} \quad + \quad \text{Sol.} \rightleftharpoons \text{Sol. } H^+ + A^-$$
Acid   Protophilic
          solvent

They are subdivided as dissociating and non-dissociating.

Weak bases in them act as differentiating solvents for acids. Strong bases act as levelling solvents for acids, as they enhance the strength of weak acids.

3. Protogenic solvents

e.g. Acetic acid, Anhydrous Sulphuric acid, Anhydrous HF. They are acidic and have protons. They tend to donate proton and thus react with bases.

They generally exert leveling effect on bases as they enhance strength of weak bases.

4. Amphiprotic solvents

e.g. Acetic acid, alcohols. They have both protophilic and protogenic properties and hence act as acids as well as bases and are capable of reacting with bases and acids. They behave as bases in presence of strong acids and behave as acids in presence of strong bases.

e.g. Acetic acid

As acid $CH_3COOH + NaOH \rightleftharpoons H_2O + CH_3COO^-Na^+ + OH^-$

Sodium salt

As base $HClO_4 + CH_3COOH \rightleftharpoons ClO_4^- + CH_3COOH_2^+$

Onium ion

Pyridine is weakly basic, but because of its poor strength it cannot be titrated vs. strong acid like perchloric acid ($HClO_4$). This can be made possible with amphiprotic solvent like acetic acid.

$$CH_3COOH + C_5H_5N \rightleftharpoons C_5H_5NH^+ + CH_3COO^-$$

Act as acid Pyridine

$$CH_3COOH \quad + \quad HClO_4 \rightleftharpoons ClO_4^- + CH_3COOH_2^+$$

Act as   Perchloric
base   acid

Thus, acetic acid acts as acid for pyridine and base for perchloric acid. But this does not affect the overall reaction because acetic acid is again formed and is not lost in reaction.

$$CH_3COO^- + CH_3COOH_2^+ \rightarrow 2CH_3COOH$$

Main reaction

$$HClO_4 + C_5H_5N \rightleftharpoons C_5H_5NH^+ + ClO_4^-$$

Therefore, it enhances basicity of pyridine so that it can be titrated vs. perchloric acid. This effect is also known as a leveling effect.

Non-aqueous solvents can also be classified as –

1.   Levelling solvents: They may be protophilic or protogenic solvents. They can be strongly acidic or strong basic. e.g. If a base is acting as leveling solvent, it levels the strength of acids added to it. It will appear that all acids in contact with that base have the same strength. E.g. Perchloric acid is a strong acid and acetic acid is a weak acid, these two acids will appear to be of the same strength in presence of a strong base. Such a base acts as a levelling solvent. It does so because it accepts all protons from both the acids. So, both acids are involved in the reaction and in the end they appear indistinguishable. It seems as if they are of the same strength.

This effect which a strong base has on strong and weak acids is called as levelling effect in which the acidity of a weak acid is enhanced and acidity of a strong acid is depressed to make them appear to be of the same strength.

Similar effect can be observed for strong acids, they will level the strength of strong and weak bases.

This is also because reaction goes to completion.

$$HX + Solvent \rightleftharpoons H^+S + X^-$$

Acid   (Base)

All of the acid takes part in reaction and gets converted into product. In this solvent strong and weak both acids are completely dissociated.

2.   Differentiating solvent: These are solvents which do not show levelling effect and tend to differentiate in strength of acids or bases. They are generally weak acids or weak bases.

e.g. If a base is acting as a differentiating solvent for two acids (strong and weak), it will make the strong acid appear more stronger and weak acid to be more weaker; which means that it will enhance acidity of the strong acid and it will decrease acidity of the weak acid.

$$HX + Solvent \rightleftharpoons H^+S + A^-$$

Acid   Base

This happens because the above reaction does not go to completion, which means that this base (differentiating solvent) is weak. As this base is weak, it is capable of accepting less number of protons, so when it is in contact with stronger and weak acids, it will prefer to take proton from strong acid which will make it appear as strong. Now that it cannot accept more protons, the weak acid will not get a chance to donate them. As the weak acid will not donate the protons, it will not appear as an acid. It may not at all take part in the reaction, so eventually strong acid has behaved as acid and weak acid has not, so this solvent has differentiated between strong and weak acid. In this solvent strong and weak acids are not completely dissociated.

Whether both acids will take part in reaction or not depends on their dissociation constants KH_A and KH_B.

Examples of Non-aqueous solvents

1.   **Glacial acetic acid:** It contains 0.1-1% water. Acetic anhydride is added to convert water to acetic acid. It can be combined with other solvents e.g. Acetonitrile

2.   **Acetonitrile:** It is used in combination with acetic acid, chloroform, phenol. It gives sharp end points for metals.

3. **Dioxan:** It is not a levelling solvent. It can be used in place of glacial acetic acid. It can be used to analyse metals.

4. **Dimethyl formamide (DMF):** It is protophilic solvent used for amides and acids but end point detection is difficult.

5. **Alcohols:** Mixtures of glycols and alcohols or glycols and hydrocarbons. e.g. ethylene glycol + propanol or butanol. They are used for salts of organic acids [soaps].

Problems with Non-aqueous solvents

1. They are toxic in nature so must be handled with care.

2. They have coefficient of cubical expansion higher than aqueous solvents.

   e.g.   Acetic acid -1.07×10^{-3} at 20°C

                   Water $- 0.21 \times 10^{-3}$ at 20°C

   It means their normality changes by 0.1% with 1°C change in temperature. Hence, temperature must be controlled during titration otherwise, strength will change.

3. They are expensive as compared to aqueous solvents.

4. Their release in the environment must be limited.

5. Solvents like acetonitrile, Dioxan must be purified before use by ion exchange resin or treatment with asbestos.

4.3 INDICATORS

1. **For titration of weak bases**

   (a) Crystal violet (Gentian violet). It is a 0.5% w/v solution in glacial acetic acid.

       Colour at basic pH is violet which changes to blue, green and then yellow in acidic pH.

   (b) pNaphthol benzein [α naphthol benzein]

       0.2% w/v in acetic acid

       Colour at basic pH is yellow which sharply changes to green at acidic pH.

   (c) Quinaldine Red – It is 0.1% w/v solution in ethanol.

       Colour at basic pH - Pink.

       Colour at acidic pH - Colourless

   (d) Malachite green

       Colour at basic pH - Green

       Colour at acidic pH - Yellow.

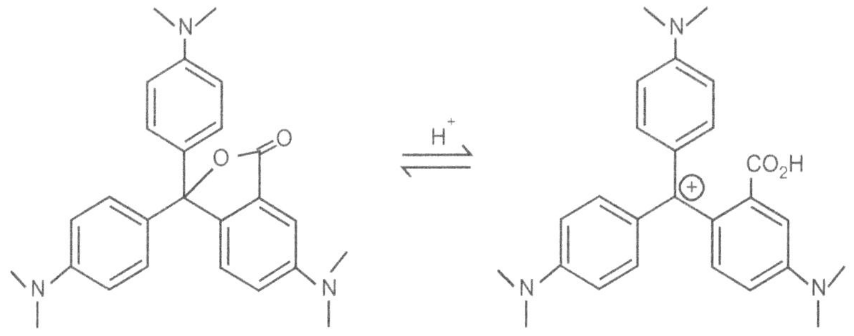

Crystal violet

2. **For titration of acids**

    (a) Thymol blue (Thymolsulfonaphthalein]

    It is 0.2% w/v solution in methanol

    Used for carboxylic acids, imides, sulfonamides, it is yellow coloured at acidic pH, and has blue colour in basic pH.

    (b) Azo violet [p-nitrobenzeneazo resorcinol]

    Used for fairly weak acids

    Colour at acidic pH - Red

    Colour at basic pH - Blue

    (c) O-nitroaniline - Used for weaker acids.

    (d) Phenolphthalein, thymolpthalein are preferred for titrations in pyridine and in alcohol.

4.4 PREPARATION AND STANDARDISATION OF PERCHLORIC ACID, 0.1 M

•   Perchloric acid is a strong acid used in non-aqueous titrations. It is a liquid and available as 72% in non-aqueous solvent.

•   **Preparation**

    Add 8.5 ml of perchloric acid slowly to 500 ml glacial acetic acid with continuous and efficient mixing. Add 30 ml acetic anhydride and adjust volume to 1000 ml with glacial acetic acid and allow it to stand for 24 hours.

Acetic anhydride is added to react with water if any. It has to be added after dilution of perchloric acid in glacial acetic acid; if it is initially mixed with perchloric acid, it forms acetyl perchlorate which is explosive. Therefore, sequence of their addition to be followed is perchloric acid then acetic acid and then acetic anhydride. The solution is kept for 24 hours, for acetic anhydride to react completely with water present in the solution.

After preparation, determination of water is carried out, it should be between 0.2-0.05%; if it exceeds this then add more amount of acetic anhydride, allow it to stand for 24 hours and carry out determination again.

- Preparation of other molarity (less than 0.1 M) solutions are done by dilution of 0.1 M perchloric acid with glacial acetic acid.

Standardisation

0.35 g of potassium hydrogen phthalate [powdered lightly and dried a 120°C for 2 hours], dissolve in 50 ml anhydrous glacial acetic acid and 0.1 ml crystal violet as indicator. Titrate with prepared 0.1 M perchloric acid until emerald green colour is obtained.

1ml as 0.1M $HClO_4 \cong 0.02041$g as potassium hydrogen phthalate.

- **Principle**

Perchloric acid is a strong acid which donates its proton to potassium hydrogen phthalate and forms phthalic acid and potassium perchlorate.

After all of the potassium hydrogen phthalate is reacted, perchloric acid reacts with the indicator, crystal violet and forms a complex which is green in colour.

4.5 KARL FISCHER TITRATION

Karl Fischer (KF) titration is a popular method of non-aqueous titration used for determination of water. In a beaker, the analyte from which water content is to be determined is taken and nitrogen gas is purged. Solution is stirred using a magnetic stirrer. Two electrodes [cathode and anode] connected by external circuit are immersed in the solution and the current is measured. From the burette KF reagent is added. During titration, cathode is polarised and anode is depolarised by iodide ions. At the end point when all water from sample has reacted with the reagent, free iodine depolarises cathode and deflection in current is observed which persists for not less than 30 seconds.

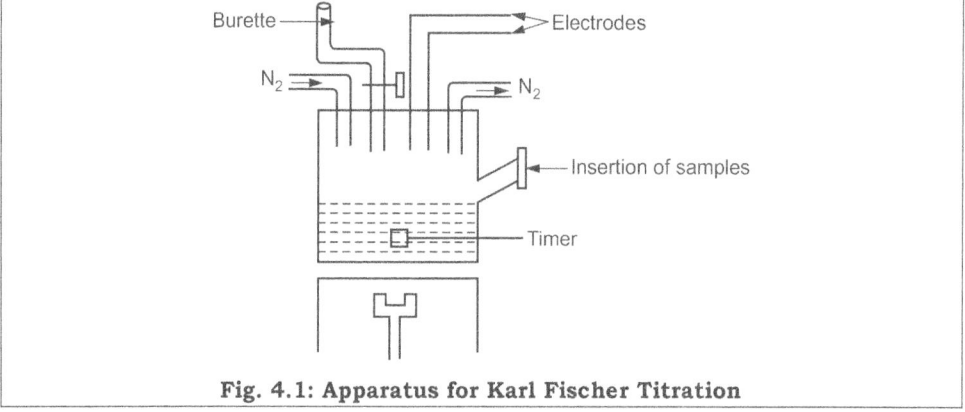

Fig. 4.1: Apparatus for Karl Fischer Titration

Principle

Iodine reacts with water molecules with the help of other reagents.

$$3C_2H_5N + SO_2 + I_2 + H_2O \rightarrow 2C_5H_5\overset{+}{N}HI + C_5H_5\overset{+}{N}SO_2O^-$$

$$C_5H_5\overset{+}{N}SO_2O^- + CH_3OH \rightarrow C_5H_5\overset{+}{N}HCH_3OSO_2O^-$$

1 ml of KF Reagent $\cong 0.1566$ mg of H_2O

Limitations/Precautions

1. Reagent is very unstable, must be prepared freshly and standardised against known water/solid sodium dihydrogen tartarate.

2. Prevent exposure to atmospheric moisture, by purging N_2 and using guard tubes filled with freshly activated silica gel.

3. Lubrication of stopcocks must be done with silicon grease and not with petroleum jelly, as it reacts with KFR.

4. Reagent is not stable to light, store in amber coloured containers.

Preparation of KFR Reagent

Take 400 ml anhydrous methanol, add 80 g of dry pyridine immersed in freezing mixture. Slowly pass SO_2 gas in cold solution with continuous agitation until weight increases by 20g. Prevent entry of moisture. Add 45g of iodine. Shake to dissolve and allow it to stand for 24 hours before use.

Have you heard about this?

Litmus paper used in the laboratory is made from water-soluble mixture of different dyes extracted from lichens, especially *Roccella tinctoria*. This mixture is absorbed on to filter paper. The resulting piece of paper or solution with water becomes a pH indicator to test materials for acidity and basicity. Neutral litmus paper is purple in colour. Blue litmus paper turns red under acidic conditions and red litmus paper turns blue under basic (i.e. alkaline) conditions, with the colour change occurring over the pH range 4.5-8.3 (at 25°C). The mixture contains 10 to 15 different dyes (Erythrolein, Azolitmin, Spaniolitmin, Leucoorcein, Leucazolitmin etc). Pure Azolitmin does show nearly the same effect as litmus. Currently the main sources are *Roccella montagnei* (Mozambique) and *Dendrographa leucophoea* (California).

The pH Scale

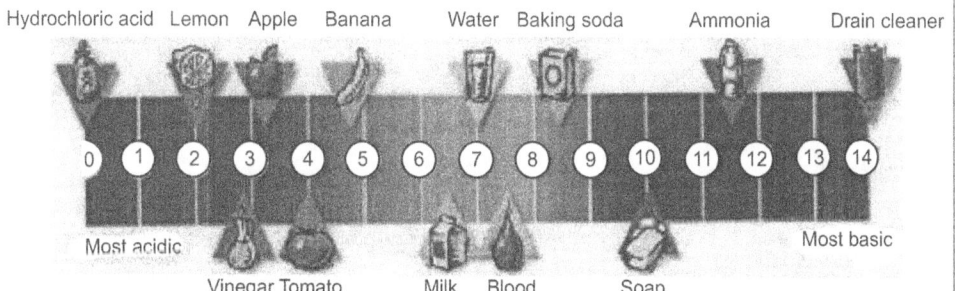

***

5

PRECIPITATION REACTIONS AND TITRATION

Precipitation

It is a process of combination of two ionic species to form an insoluble product.

For using precipitation in titration, the following conditions must be fulfilled.

1. Precipitate must be practically insoluble in the solvent employed for titration.

2. Formation of precipitate should be rapid and quantitative.

3. Titration results should not be hampered by adsorption of ions on precipitate.

4. It should be possible to detect the end point of the titration.

5.1 SOLUBILITY OF SLIGHTLY SOLUBLE SALTS

Solubility product: Product of molar ionic concentrations of an electrolyte is called as its solubility product (K_{sp}).

$$BA_{solid} \rightleftharpoons B^+ + A^-$$

$$K_{sp} = [B^+][A^-]$$

K_{sp} is constant for a given solute in a particular solvent and at a particular temperature. From this, concentration of one of the ion can be calculated if the other is known.

e.g. K_{sp} of $MgCO_3$ = 4×10^{-6} = $[Mg^{2+}] [CO_3^{2-}]$

$Mg(OH)_2$ = 6×10^{-10} = $[Mg^{2+}] [OH^-]$

Therefore, K_{sp} is the concentration product which keeps ions in dissolved form. Ionic concentration less than or equal to K_{sp} leads to solubilisation of electrolyte. When concentration of ions present in solution exceeds K_{sp}, precipitation occurs.

e.g. $Mg(OH_2)$ will precipitate when product of molar concentrations of Mg^{2+} and OH^- will be greater than 6×10^{-10}.

There is one phenomenon known as common ion effect. It states that solubility of any slightly soluble salt can be decreased [salt will get precipitated] by adding an excess of either of its own ions [common ion]. So, by addition of common ion of salt, it is forced to get precipitated. It happens because addition of one of the ions in excess increases the ionic product which when exceeds the solubility product results in precipitation.e.g.For precipitation of $Mg(OH)_2$, excess of either $Mg^{2+}(MgCO_3)$ or $OH^-(KOH)$ is added.

Factors affecting solubility

1. Ionic concentration/common ion effect

When concentration product of reacting species exceeds K_{sp}, solubility decreases.

2. pH

Solubility increases by decrease in pH if anion of the salt is the conjugate base of a weak acid.

$$CH_3COONa \rightleftharpoons CH_3COO^- + Na^+ \qquad\qquad ... (1)$$

Salt   Anion   Cation

$$CH_3COOH \rightleftharpoons CH_3COO^- + H^+ \qquad\qquad ... (2)$$

Weak acid   Conjugate base

So, solubility of CH_3COONa, will be enhanced at acidic pH. At acidic pH, as there will be more H^+ ions they will force equilibrium (2) towards left and equilibrium (1) towards right. So its solubility is increased.

Solubility increases by increase in pH if cation of salt is conjugate acid of a weak base.

5.2

3. Temperature

With a few exceptions, rise in temperature causes increase in solubility of salt.

	AgCl	BaSO$_4$
e.g. 10°C	1.72 mg/L	2.2 mg/ L
100°C	21.1 mg/ L	3.9 mg/ L

4. Solvent

Addition of organic solvents [methanol, ethanol] generally reduces solubility.

Fractional precipitation

When a salt solution contains two ions, both of which are capable of forming slightly soluble salts with same ion, fractional precipitation of both ions is likely to occur, complete precipitation of any one of the ion may be achieved by controlling concentration of other ion.

e.g. $AgNO_3$ can form precipitate with Cl^-, I^-, Br^-.

$$K_{sp} \text{ AgCl} = 1.2 \times 10^{-10}$$

$$K_{sp} \text{ AgI} = 1.7 \times 10^{-16}$$

$$K_{sp} \text{ AgBr} = 3.5 \times 10^{-13}$$

As K_{sp} of AgI is less, in a solution containing Cl^- and I^-, when $AgNO_3$ is added, AgI starts precipitating first when $[Ag^+]$ exceeds $\dfrac{1.7 \times 10^{-16}}{[I^-]}$.

AgCl starts precipitating when $[Ag^+]$ exceeds $\dfrac{1.2 \times 10^{-10}}{Cl^-}$.

After this, both ions will precipitate simultaneously. Ag^+ will be in equilibrium with both salts.

$$[Ag^+] = \frac{K_{sp} \text{ (AgI)}}{[I^-]} = \frac{K_{sp} \text{ (AgCl)}}{[Cl^-]}$$

$$\frac{[I^-]}{[Cl^-]} = \frac{K_{sp} \text{ (AgI)}}{K_{sp} \text{ (AgCl)}} = \frac{1.7 \times 10^{-16}}{1.2 \times 10^{-10}} = 1.4 \times 10^{-6} \text{ or } \frac{1}{1.4 \times 10^6}$$

Similarly, $\quad \dfrac{[I^-]}{[Br^-]} = \dfrac{K_{sp} \text{ (AgI)}}{K_{op} \text{ (AgBr)}} = \dfrac{1.7 \times 10^{-16}}{3.5 \times 10^{-13}} = \dfrac{1}{2 \times 10^3}$

So complete precipitation of AgI will occur and AgCl and AgBr will start precipitating when concentration of Cl^- and Br^- is greater than I^- ions by 1.4×10^6 times and 2×10^3 times respectively.

As concentration difference is greater in Cl^- and I^- than Br^- and I^- complete precipitation is possible in the first case than the second. Complete precipitation point is detected by use of adsorption indicator or by potentiometry.

5.2 TITRATION CURVES

If precipitation is rapid, complete and quantitative, ionic concentration plotted vs. volume of titrant gives sigmoidal curve, where point of inflection represents end point.

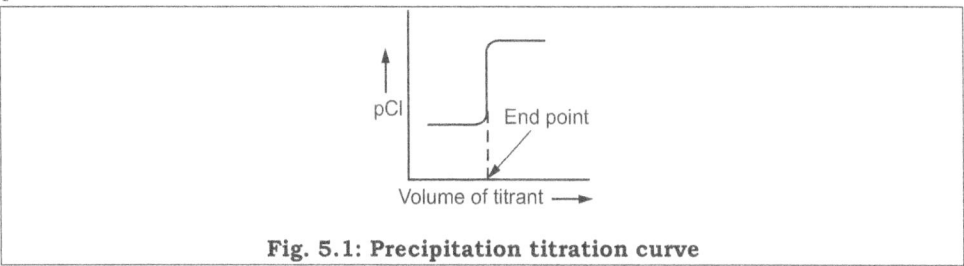

Fig. 5.1: Precipitation titration curve

Initially, concentration of Cl^- ions is high [−log is low] which decreases gradually and PCl rises suddenly at end point.

e.g. 100 ml, 0.1 M NaCl vs. 0.1 M AgNO$_3$, expected end point is 100 ml.

1. **Initial concentration of Cl^-**

$$Cl^- = \frac{\text{Volume of NaCl} \times \text{Molarity of NaCl}}{\text{Total volume}}$$

$$= \frac{100 \times 0.1}{100} = 0.1$$

$_p$Cl = Negative log of concentration of Cl^-

$_p$Cl = -log 0.1 = 1

2. **After addition of 50 ml of AgNO$_3$**

$$NaCl + AgNO_3 \rightarrow AgCl \downarrow + NaNO_3$$

$$Cl^- = \frac{50 \times 0.1}{150}$$

$$= 0.033$$

$_p$C = 1.48

3. **After addition of 90 ml of AgNO$_3$**

$$Cl^- = \frac{10 \times 0.1}{190} = 0.0052$$

$_p$Cl = 2.32

4. **At equivalence point**

$$Cl^- = Ag^+ = \frac{1}{2} \, pk_{sp} \, AgCl = 4.96$$

$$= \frac{1}{2} \times \log 1.2 \times 10^{-10}$$

---

5. **After equivalence point** $= \dfrac{10 \times 0.1}{210} = 5.16$

So pCl rises gradually before and after end point, sudden rise is seen at end point.

5.3 DETECTION OF END POINT/ INDICATORS INCLUDING FAJAN'S METHOD

When precipitation reaction is complete between analyte and titrant, there must be a suitable means to indicate it.

1. **Formation of a coloured precipitate**

Here internal indicator is added such that it is capable of forming precipitate with the titrant. When all of the analyte has reacted with titrant, extra drop of titrant reacts with indicator to form a precipitate.

Free indicator must have different colour than its precipitate.

e.g. Potassium chromate, in Mohr's method.

$$K_2CrO_4 \quad + \quad 2AgNO_3 \rightarrow Ag_2CrO_4 \downarrow + 2KNO_3$$

Colourless   Excess after   Red ppt

analyte reaction

$$K_{sp} \text{ of } Ag_2CrO_4 = 1.7 \times 10^{-12}$$

$$K_{sp} \text{ of } AgCl = 1.2 \times 10^{-10}$$

Ideally in the beginning of titration when both NaCl and K_2CrO_4 are present and $AgNO_3$ is added, it is expected that the precipitate will form which has a lower solubility product, because its Ksp is exceeded first i.e. Ag_2CrO_4 must precipitate giving immediate red colour. But as concentration of indicator is very low as compared to analyte (NaCl), it does not form at that point. Red precipitate is obtained only after all AgCl has precipitated.

But this indicator cannot be used in acidic pH.

$$2CrO_4^{2-} + 2H^+ \rightleftharpoons 2HCrO_4^-$$

At acidic pH, it reacts with H^+ ions and is not available to react with titrant to show colour change.

It is used for determination of Cl^- and Br^- but not for I^- and SCN^-, because I^- and SCN^- when precipitated as AgI and AgSCN strongly adsorb chromate ions, giving false indistinct end point.

2.   Formation of soluble coloured compound

Here, when all of analyte has reacted, titrant reacts with indicator to form a soluble coloured complex.

Free indicator must have a different colour than its complex at the end point.

e.g. Ferric ammonium sulphate in Volhard's method, $AgNO_3$ is added in excess to halide solution (X^-) and is back titrated vs. NH_4SCN.

$$AgNO_3 + X^- \rightleftharpoons AgX \downarrow + NO_3^-$$

$$AgNO_3 + SCN^- \rightleftharpoons AgSCN \downarrow + NO_3^-$$

When all $AgNO_3$ has reacted with SCN^-, extra drop of SCN^- reacts with indicator.

$$Fe^{+++} + SCN^- \rightleftharpoons [FeSCN]^{2+}$$
$$\text{Reddish brown}$$
$$\text{colour}$$
$$\text{ferrous thiocyanate}$$

$$K_{sp} \text{ AgCl} = 1.2 \times 10^{-10}$$

$$K_{sp} \text{ AgSCN} = 7.1 \times 10^{-13}$$

As $[FeSCN]^{2+}$ is not a precipitate, it does not have K_{sp}.

This ferric ammonium sulphate hydrolyses in basic pH; moreover silver ions form AgOH at alkaline pH, therefore acidic pH is used for titration.

When this indicator is to be used for determination of iodide, it should be added after complete precipitation of AgI. Because I^- has tendency to react with indicator and reduce it to give premature end point.

$$AgNO_3 + I^- \rightarrow AgI + NO_3^-$$

$$2Fe^{3+} + 2I^- \rightleftharpoons 2Fe^{2+} + I_2$$

3.   K Fajan's method/Use of adsorption indicators

Some indicators get adsorbed on precipitate of analyte preferentially after end point thus marking the end point of the titration. Indicator should have a different colour in free form and should impart different colour to precipitate when it is adsorbed on it.

Acidic dyes: Fluorescein, Eosin.

Basic dyes: Rhodamine.

Such indication is possible because colloidal precipitates has tendency to adsorb its own ions. e.g.

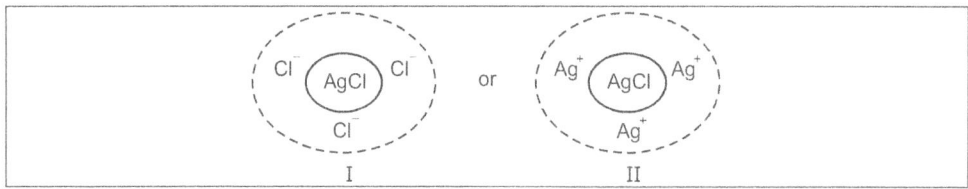

I   II

When $AgNO_3$ is added in the analyte NaCl, precipitate of AgCl is formed. As concentration of Cl^- is high compared to Ag^+, it adsorbs on the precipitate preferntially[because $AgNO_3$ is added dropwise from the burette].

Thus condition I is more favourable. Also, there is an excess of Na^+ in the solution and as it has a charge opposite to the primary layer [Cl^-] it immediately adsorbs as a secondary layer.

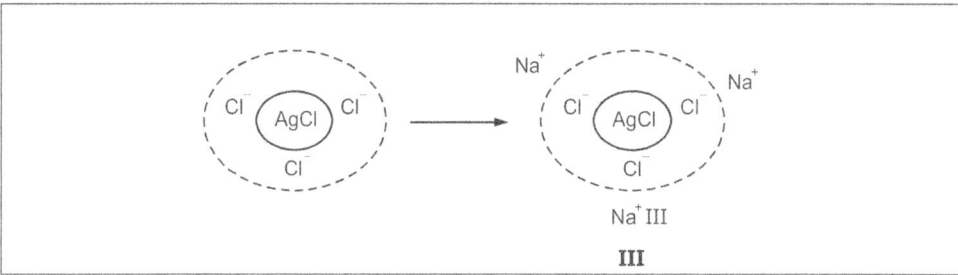

Na^+ III

III

After end point, when all of Cl^- has reacted, there is positive primary layer.

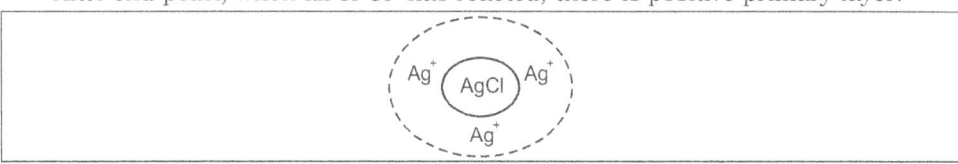

It should be noted that Na^+ is also present in solution but it cannot adsorb as primary layer because AgCl can only adsorb its own ions [Ag^+ or Cl^-]. Now on such primary positive layer, second layer can be either NO_3^- or indicator anion.

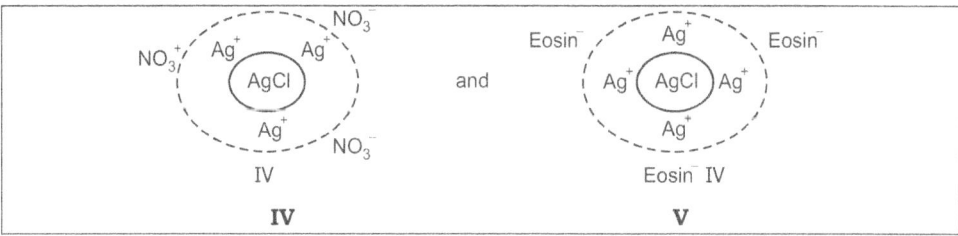

IV   and   Eosin$^-$ IV

IV   **V**

Such adsorbed indicator has different colour and hence it shows colour change at the end point of titration. But it is sensitive to light, hence must be carried out in minimum exposure to light.

e.g. Fluorescein shows pink colour when adsorbed and yellow green colour in free anion form.The choice of indicator depends on the following.

1. Its charge must be opposite to the charge of the ion of the titrant.

2. It should be adsorbed secondarily only after the end point.

3. Precipitate should be colloidal in nature.

Flurescein is a very weak acid, its Na salt is used and as it is a weak acid's salt its ionisation is very poor at acidic pH. Hence, it is used in alkaline pH.

Q. Why eosin is used at acidic pH

Eosin

Eosin is tetrabromofluorescein and it is used as its Na salt. As it is stronger acid than fluorescein, ionisation/dissociation [we need anion of indicator to show end point] of its sodium salt is not affected by pH and hence it can be used at acidic pH even near to 2.

The only problem with eosin is that it is more strongly adsorbed than Cl^- so cannot be used in its determination. Because we need indicator anion to adsorb only after end point and as secondary layer, it should be less strongly adsorbed than analyte ion. Eosin is less strongly adsorb than Br^-, I^-, SCN^- and hence can be used for their estimation.

4. Gay Lussac's method/Turbidimetry method

Precipitation involves reaction of analyte and titrant to form an insoluble precipitate which gives rise to turbidity in solution.

Therefore, as long as analyte is present, precipitate gets formed and turbidity keeps on increasing. When all of the analyte completely reacts with titrant, extra addition of titrant does not produce more precipitate, so that can be taken as end point. Burette reading when there is no further increase in turbidity is end point.

This can be visually observed or by instrumentally measured.

Visual detection involves careful observation of production of precipitate. In addition, precipitate must be settled down or coagulated to ensure that there is completion of precipitation.

As slowly with addition of titrant, there is production of more and more precipitate, turbidity rises. Nepheloturbidometer can be used to measure turbidity. So turbidity will increase with addition of titrant and when reaction is complete there is no further rise in turbidity thus marking end point.

B.R.	Turbidity
0	0
1	10
3	15
5	20
7	25
9	30
10	30
12	30

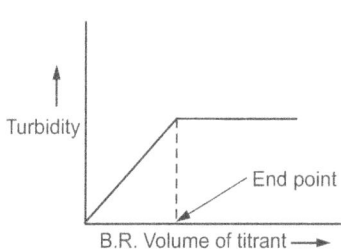

Fig. 5.2: Turbidimetry Method

In instrumental detection, solution must be uniformly shaken after addition of titrant (1 ml at a time) and turbidity is measured.

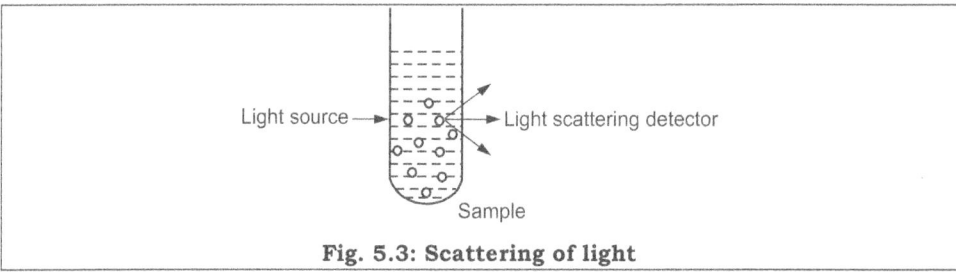

Fig. 5.3: Scattering of light

Measurement of turbidity is based on scattering on radiation by particles of precipitate.

5.4 ARGENTOMETRIC TITRATIONS

Titrations involving use of silver nitrate are called as argentometric titrations.

• These are used for determination of chlorides and bromides in neutral solution. A typical example of this kind is the **Mohr's method**.

• Potassium chromate is used as an indicator.

- Halides and chromate both are capable of forming precipitate with silver, however AgCl precipitates first because chloride ions are in excess than chromate ions.

$$K_{sp} \text{ AgCl} = 1.2 \times 10^{-10}$$

$$K_{sp} \text{ Ag}_2\text{CrO}_4 = 1.7 \times 10^{-12}$$

- When all of chloride reacts with AgNO$_3$, at equivalence point extra drop of AgNO$_3$ reacts with indicator.

$$\text{NaCl} + \text{AgNO}_3 \rightarrow \text{AgCl} \downarrow + \text{NaNO}_3$$

$$\text{K}_2\text{CrO}_4 + 2\text{AgNO}_3 \rightarrow \text{Ag}_2\text{CrO}_4 \downarrow + 2\text{KNO}_3$$

Red Precipitate

- It can also be applied to bromides in a similar way.

- These titrations need to be performed in neutral or slightly alkaline solution (pH 6.5-9), because in acidic condition protonation of chromate ions decrease the concentration of indicators ions.

$$2\text{CrO}_4^{2-} + 2\text{H}^+ \rightleftharpoons 2\text{HCrO}_4^-$$

As concentration of indicator ions will get reduced, its solubility product will never be exceeded and red precipitate will not get formed. At highly alkaline pH silver hydroxide gets formed and precipitated in brown black colour.

5.5 TITRATIONS INVOLVING AMMONIUM AND POTASSIUM THIOCYANATE

- These are titrations in which AgNO$_3$ is added in excess to the halide solution and remaining AgNO$_3$ is back titrated vs. ammonium or potassium thiocyanate.

- Such titrations are called as indirect argentiometry or **Volhard's method**.

- Ferric ammonium sulphate is used as indicator which forms reddish brown coloured solution at end point [extra drop of thiocyanate reacts with indicator to form ferrous thiocyanate].

1. $\quad$ $\text{NaCl} + \text{AgNO}_3 \rightarrow \text{AgCl} \downarrow + \text{NaNO}_3$

2. $\quad$ $\text{AgNO}_3 + \text{NH}_4\text{SCN} \rightarrow \text{AgSCN} \downarrow + \text{NH}_4\text{NO}_3$

3. $\quad$ $\text{Fe}^{+++} + \text{SCN}^- \rightarrow [\text{FeSCN}]^{2+}$

Ferrous thiocyanate

- It suffers from a drawback of adsorption of silver ions on a precipitate of AgCl giving inaccurate burette readings. It can be prevented/minimised by performing rapid titration, boiling and removing precipitate by filtration, adding KNO_3 to coagulate the precipitate or adding immiscible liquids like nitrobenzene, to coat the precipitate.

- It is generally performed at acidic pH.

- Titrations of iodides, thiocyanates which were not possible by Mohr's method can be performed by this method.

5.6 MOHR'S METHOD AND VOLHARDS METHOD

Mohr's Method	Volhard's method
1. It is a direct titration method where halide solution is titrated vs. standard $AgNO_3$	1. It is indirect/back titration where excess of $AgNO_3$ is added to halide solution and back titrated vs. NH_4SCN.
2. Indicator - K_2CrO_4 potassium dichromate/chromate	2. Indicator - Ferric ammonium sulphate.
3. End point is formation of red precipitate of silver chromate $AgCrO_4$.	3. End point is formation of red coloured complex solution of $(FeSCN)^{2+}$.
4. Mechanism (a) $Cl^- + AgNO_3 \rightarrow AgCl \downarrow$ (white ppt) (b) $AgNO_3 + CrO_4^{2-} \rightarrow 2Ag_2CrO_4 \downarrow$ Red ppt $K_{sp}AgCl = 1.2 \times 10^{-10}$ $K_{sp}Ag_2CrO_4 = 1.7 \times 10^{-12}$ AgCl precipitates first because of high concentration of Cl^-. No need of boiling, filtration or addition of any reagent.	4. Mechanism (a) $Cl^- + AgNO_3 \rightarrow AgCl \downarrow$ (white precipitate) (b) $AgNO_3 + NH_4SCN \rightarrow AgSCN \downarrow$ $+ NH_4NO_3$ (c) $Fe^{+++} + SCN^- \rightleftharpoons [FeSCN]^{2+}$ Ferrous thiocyanate $K_{sp}AgCl = 1.2 \times 10^{-10}$ $K_{sp}AgSCN = 7.1 \times 10^{-13}$ $\dfrac{Cl^-}{SCN^-} = 169 \quad \dfrac{Br^-}{SCN^-} = 0.5$ At equilibrium, as ratio is 169, excess of NH_4SCN reacts with AgCl.

Mohr's Method	Volhard's method
	AgCl + NH₄SCN → AgSCN + Cl⁻ $$AgCl + NH_4SCN \rightarrow AgSCN + Cl^-$$ Giving high burette reading. Also Ag^+ can adsorb on precipitate of AgCl, so AgCl need to be removed or covered. (a) Perform rapid titration. (b) Boil and remove precipitate by filtration. (c) Add KNO_3 which coagulates precipitate and filter, it also desorbs Ag^+. (d) Coat precipitate by immiscible liquid. e.g. Nitrobenzene.
5. pH should be neutral or slightly alkaline. At acidic pH. $$2CrO_4^{2-} + 2H^+ \rightleftharpoons HCrO_4^-$$ This reduces indicator concentration. At alkaline pH. AgOH forms precipitate which is brown black in colour.	5. pH should be acidic, hence K_2CrO_4 cannot be used as indicator.
6. Example: Standardisation of $AgNO_3$.	6. Example: Assay of NaCl.
7. Application: Determination of Cl^-, Br^- in neutral solution.	7. Application: Determination of Br^-, I^-, Cl^- in acidic solution.
8. Titration of I^- and SCN^- is not possible because they adsorb on chromate ions.	8. I^- can be titrated without error.

Have you heard about them?

Karl **Friedrich Mohr** (November 4, 1806 – September 28, 1879) was a German chemist famous for his early statement of the principle of the conservation of energy. He proposed direct titrations with silver nitrate today known as Mohr's method.

Mohr was the leading scientific chemist of his time in Germany, and the inventor of many improvements in analytical methodology. He invented laboratory apparatus such as Pinchcock, Cork borer, Mohr's balance. Ammonium iron (II) sulfate, $(NH_4)_2Fe (SO_4)_2 \cdot 6H_2O$, is named as Mohr's salt after him. He invented an improved burette which had a tip at the bottom and a clamp (a 'Mohr's clip'). He took one of his own pipettes; he added a short length of rubber tubing at the bottom pinched by a brass clip of his own design. Squeezing the clip, the reagent could be delivered continuously or drop wise, while the scale could be read at a glance. His application to the details of practical pharmacy and of chemical operations, his wonderful skill and inventive mind, resulted in the improvement and completion of old and in the construction of a large number of novel apparatus, appliances, and processes in pharmacy and chemical analysis.

Jacob Volhard (4 June 1834-14 January 1910) was the German chemist. Volhard is best known for his development of volumetric analysis, notably the titration of silver with ammonium thiocyanate, but he also known for synthesis of creatine in 1868.

He was born in Darmstadt and he studied chemistry at Giessen under his fellow Darmstadter Justus von Liebig, whom he followed to Munich. After working in London (under Hofmann) and Marburg (under Kolbe), he became Professor of Organic Chemistry at Munich, briefly at Erlangen and finally in Halle. He discovered together with his student Hugo Erdmann, the Volhard-Erdmann cyclization reaction. He was also responsible for the improvement of the Hell-Volhard-Zelinsky halogenation.

6

COMPLEXOMETRIC REACTIONS AND TITRATION

6.1 Introduction

6.2 Stability of Complexes

6.3 Chelating Agents

6.4 Theory of Complexometric Titrations

6.5 Metallochromic (pM) Indicators

6.6 Types of Complexometric Titrations

6.7 Titration curve

6.8 Disodium EDTA

6.1 INTRODUCTION

1. Complex: It consists of one or more molecules bound to a central (metal) ion. Agent which forms a complex is called as a complexing agent.

2. Ligand: Ligands are molecules which bind to metals and form a complex or any electron donating ion or molecule.e.g. Ammonia is also known as a ligand. Ligands generally bind through amino and carboxylate groups.

3. Werners co-ordination number/co-ordination number: Maximum number of groups/molecules that can be bound to metal ion is known as its coordination number. It is characteristic of a metal ion. It depends on steric factors and not on valency and ion. e.g. for elements in 2nd period of periodic table, it is 4. For elements in 3rd period of periodic table, it is 6.

For Tungsten and molybdenum, it is 8.

4.   Types of Ligands: The different types of ligands are summarised below.

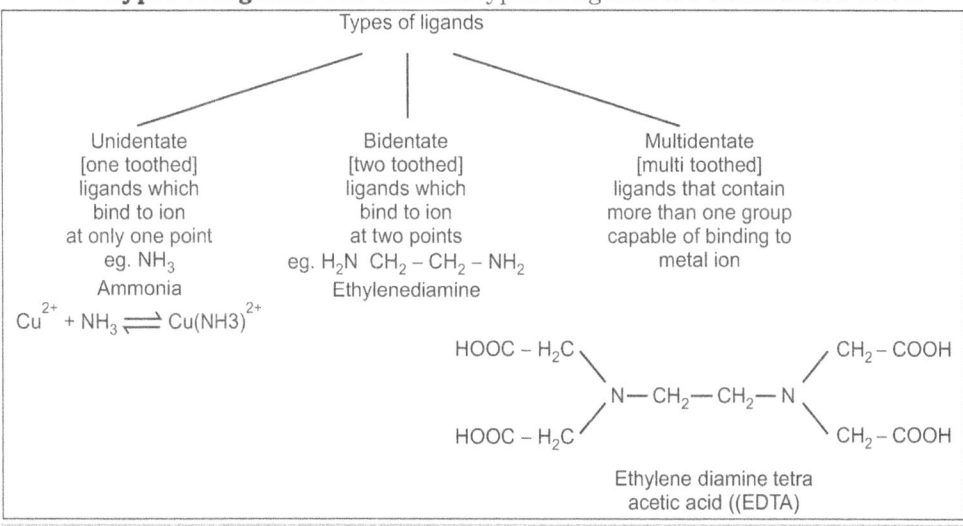

6.2 STABILITY OF COMPLEXES

$$M \quad + \quad Y \quad \rightleftharpoons \quad MY$$

Metal   Complexing   Complex

Agent

$$K = \frac{[MY]}{[M][Y]}$$

K = Stability constant/Formation constant

$\frac{1}{K}$ = Instability constant/Dissociation constant

e.g. Ca - EDTA complex, K = 2.5×10^{11}, log K_a = 10.96.

Higher the value of K, more is the stability. For Pb, log K = 18.04.

For successful titration, log of stability constant should be greater than 8.

Li, Na does form complexes with EDTA that have very weak stability constant and therefore not possible to titrate.

Ag, Ba complex have stability constants below 8. e.g. Ba, log K = 7.76.

Fe^{3+}, Cu^{2+} form stable but highly coloured complexes which interfere in visual detection of end point.

Factors affecting Stability of Complex

1.   pH

pH affects dissociation and pK_a values.

It can be well explained by example of EDTA.

- It has 4 protons and it is designated as H_4Y. Everytime when it forms bond, it looses one proton and acquires a negative charge.

$$H_4Y \overset{K_1}{\rightleftharpoons} H_3Y^- + H^+ \qquad pK_1 = 2$$

$$H_3Y^- \overset{K_2}{\rightleftharpoons} H_2Y^{2-} + H^+ \qquad pK_2 = 2.67$$

$$H_2Y^{2-} \overset{K_3}{\rightleftharpoons} HY^{3-} + H^+ \qquad pK_3 = 6.16$$

$$HY^{3-} \overset{K_4}{\rightleftharpoons} Y^{4-} + H^+ \qquad pK_4 = 10.26$$

As we can see, initially pK value is low (2) and then it rises, means it becomes a weaker acid as protons are lost. Dissociation of weak acid depends greatly on pH. Acid is unionised at acidic pH and onized at basic pH. Therefore, pH at which titration is performed affects complex formation and stability. If pH is very high, more dissociation will occur and Y^{4-} will exist. At acidic and neutral pH, EDTA exist as H_4Y, H_3Y^-, H_2Y^{2-}, HY^{3-}.

$$[Y'] = [H_4Y] + [H_3Y^-] + [H_2Y^{2-}] + [HY^{3-}] + [Y^{4-}]$$

$$K = \frac{[MY^{+n-4}]}{[M^{n+}] [Y^{4-}]} \qquad\qquad K' = \frac{[MY^{+n-4}]}{[M^{n+}] [Y']}$$

At high pH   At acid and neutral pH

So pH must be controlled K' = Conditional constant

2. Temperature

Increase in temperature causes slight increase in ionisation of complex, thus lowering of stability constant.

3. Presence of electrolytes/Neutral salts e.g. NaCl

Electrolytes with no ion common with complex decreases stability constant.

4. Presence of organic solvents e.g. Ethanol

They suppress ionisation of complex and thus increase stability constant.

6.3 CHELATING AGENTS

Ligands that form ring compound as a complex with ions are chelating agents. Such a ring complex is called as a chelate. It is possible for metal ion and multidentate ligand. e.g. EDTA, ethylene diamine.

Sequestering agents: Ligand which form water soluble complex with bi or poly valent metal ions are sequestering agents. e.g. EDTA.

Some complexing agents form water insoluble complexes.

e.g. Dimethyglyoxime, salicylaldoxime.

Properties of Complex

1. Generally metals form complexes.

2. Free metals and their complexes have different properties. e.g.a metal may get precipitated by certain agents while its complex may not.

3. Greater the stability of the complex, more is the difference between the properties of metal and its complexes.

6.4 THEORY OF COMPLEXOMETRIC TITRATIONS

*   In complexometric titrations, titrant (Y) and indicator (I) are selected such that both of them are capable of forming a complex with metal (M) ion to be analysed.

*   Attention should be paid to the fact that stability of metal-indicator complex is less than metal-titrant complex at the pH of the titration.

$$M \; + \; Y \; \rightleftharpoons MY \qquad\qquad \text{Reaction I}$$

Titrant   Complex

$$M \; + \; I \rightleftharpoons MI \qquad\qquad \text{Reaction II}$$

Metal indicator   Complex

*   Indicator should have a different colour in free form and in complexed form.

e.g. Mordant black II at pH 10

$$M \; + \; I \; \rightleftharpoons MI$$
$$\text{Free} \quad \text{Complex}$$
$$\text{blue} \qquad \text{pink}$$

*   Initially metal ion solution is taken in the conical flask and indicator is added. Indicator forms complex with small amount of metal ion and therefore has a specific colour. **(Reaction II)**

*   Now as titration is started, titrant starts forming complex with free metal ions. **(Reaction I)**

*   When all free metal ions are complexed with titrant, addition of more titrant breaks metal indicator complex to liberate free indicator which now has a different colour; thus end point is detected.

• It also liberates free metal ion with which titrant forms a complex. Reaction is complete as all of metal is now reacted with the titrant. (**Reaction III**)

$$MI + Y \rightleftharpoons MY + I \hspace{4cm} \text{Reaction II}$$

6.5 METALLOCHROMIC (pM) INDICATORS

Complexometric indicators/Metallochromic indicators are used to detect the end point of a titration.

Principle: Initially, metal and indicator form complex, during titration EDTA reacts with free metal. At the end point EDTA breaks metal indicator complex releasing free indicator to obtain colour change.

$$M - In + EDTA \rightarrow M\text{-EDTA} + In$$

Criteria for pM indicator

1. It must form a stable complex with metal, whose stability is less than metal-EDTA complex.

2. Indicator must have different colour in free form and in complexed form at pH of titration.

3. Colour change must be specific.

4. It must be sensitive to metal ions to give colour change.

Therefore, indicator must also be a chelating agent like EDTA, possessing several ligands to form complex with metals.

e.g.

Blue (pH 10)
free form
Mordant black II

Pink
complexed form

Mordant black II also called as Erichrome black T or solochrome black. It has two phenolic hydrogens which are ionisable with $pK_1 = 6.3$ and $pK_2 = 11.55$.

$$H_2I^- \rightleftharpoons HI^{2-} \rightleftharpoons I^{3-}$$

Red   Blue   Orange

At pH 8-10, HI^{2-} form is present, and is considered as free form of indicator. When it is complexed, it forms pink colour. So end point at pH 10 is pink to blue.

Below pH 6.3 and above pH 11.5, dye has reddish colour in free as well as in complexed form, so cannot be used.

Table 6.1: Metallochromic indicators

No.	Name	Metal ions	pH	Colour changes (complexed → free)
1.	Murexide	Cu^{2+}, Ni^{2+}, Co^{2+}, Ca^{2+}	10-11	Yellow → Blue (Ni^{2+}) Orange → Blue (Cu^{2+}) Red → Blue (Ca^{2+})
2.	Mordant black II	Mg^{2+}, Mn^{2+}, Zn^{2+}, Cd^{2+}, Hg^{2+}, Pb^{2+}, Ca^{2+}	10	Red → Blue
3.	Xylenol orange	Bi^{3+}, Th^{4+}, Zn^{2+}, Co^{2+}, Cd^{2+}, Pb^{2+}, Sn^{2+}, Ni^{2+}, Mn^{2+}	1-2 4-6	Red → Lemon yellow
4.	Methyl thymol blue	Ba^{2+}, Th^{4+}, Zi^{2+}, Hf^{4+}, Hg^{2+}, Zn^{2+}, Co^{2+}, Cd^{2+}	0-2	Blue → Yellow Blue → Colourless
		Al^{3+}, Ni^{2+}, Mn^{2+}	4-6	Blue → Orange red
		Ca^{2+}, Sr^{2+}, Ba^{2+}, Mg^{2+}	12	

Less common indicators are Calcon, catechol and violet alizarin fluoride blue.

6.6 TYPES OF COMPLEXOMETRIC TITRATIONS

1. Direct Titration

Here metal ion [e.g. $MgSO_4$] is directly titrated vs. complexing agent [EDTA] at the desired pH [e.g. 10] maintained by a suitable buffer [e.g. Ammonia buffer] using a suitable indicator [e.g. Mordant black II] till colour change [e.g. pink to blue] is obtained.

Initially metal indicator complex is formed [pink] in small amount, addition of EDTA causes metal-EDTA complex to form. When all free metal reacts with EDTA, extra drop of EDTA breaks metal-indicator complex and reacts with the liberated metal. Indicator is now free and acquires blue colour.

Precipitation of metal hydroxide can be prevented by addition of tartarate/citrate salts.

Examples of metals which can be directly titrated $-Fe^{3+}$, Ca^{2+}, Mg^{2+}, Zn^{2+}, Cd^{2+}, Cu^{2+}, Ni^{2+}, CO^{2+}, Pb^{2+}, Ba^{2+}, Mn^{2+}, Hg^{2+}, Al^{3+}.

2. Back titration

It is used for those metals which get precipitated as hydroxide, [complex in insoluble in solvent employed], for titrations where suitable indicator is not available and where rate of formation of metal-EDTA complex is very low.

Here excess of complexing agent [EDTA] is added to analyte and excess of EDTA remaining after its complex reaction with metal is titrated back with standard metal.

e.g. Analyte – Al^{3+}.

Add excess of 0.01 M EDTA and ammonia solution to adjust pH 7-8. Boil to complete complexation, cool, adjust pH to 9-8.

Indicator - Solochrome black - Potassium nitrate [Mordant black II].

End point - Blue - Pink.

Titrate remaining EDTA vs. 0.01 M $ZnSO_4$.

Now here, initially metal indicator complex will not form because, EDTA is in excess, so it reacts with all of metal. In addition, its stability constant is more than the metal-indicator complex. Therefore, indicator is free [Blue]. Now excess of EDTA reacts with metal which is added from the burette i.e. $ZnSO_4$. So Zn forms complex with EDTA, when all EDTA has reacted with Zn^{2+}, extra drop of Zn^{2+} will react with indicator [pink] colour. So colour change is opposite to that obtained in direct titration.

e.g. metals that can be back titrated - Pb^{2+}, Al^{3+}, Hg^{2+}, Ni^{2+}.

It is also applicable for metals which are in the form of their insoluble salts.

e.g. $BaSO_4$ is dissolved in ammonical EDTA and back titrated against standard $MgSO_4$.

3. Replacement/Substitution titrations

It is used when end point of titration is unsatisfactory. e.g. Ca^{2+} when titrated with EDTA, using Mordant black II. Initially, it does form complex with indicator, but it is unstable and immediately breaks to release free indicator giving colour change.

Magnesium forms stable complex with indicator, so it is used in assay of calcium.

Initial phase Ca + Mg in the analyte

Indicator added   Ca + Mg-In   (pink colour because indicator is not free).

During titration   EDTA-Ca + Mg In (Pink).

When all Ca is finished reacting, EDTA reacts with Mg. when all free Mg has reacted, ig Mg and releases free indicator.

Mg-In + Ca-EDTA + EDTA $\rightleftharpoons$ Mg-EDTA + Ca-EDTA + In Free (blue)

Mg is added in the form of $MgSO_4$ or $MgCl_2$ during precipitation of analyte solution. Its volume shall be subtracted from the burette reading is obtained.

Such replacement titrations are also performed for Pb, Hg and Fe^{3+}.

4. Alkalimetric titrations

EDTA has 4 protons, which are released when EDTA starts forming bond with metals. These released protons can be titrated with suitable alkali and an indirect measure of complex formation can be established.

$$H_4Y + M \rightleftharpoons H^+ + MH_3Y^-$$
EDTA
$$MH_3Y^- + M \rightleftharpoons M_2H_2Y^{2-} + H^+$$
$$M_2H_2Y^{2-} + M \rightleftharpoons M_3HY^{3-} + H^+$$
$$M_3HY^3 + M \rightleftharpoons M_4Y_4 + H^+$$
$$H^+ + NaOH \longrightarrow H_2O + Na^+$$

5. Titrations involving masking and demasking

EDTA has a tendency to form complex with all metals, thus it lacks selectivity. So metals from solvents, impurities also get complexed in titration thus giving misleading results.

It is also difficult in analysis of mixtures of metals. Hence, masking is done to remove interference of metals other than that of interest, which is later on demasked [set free to react].

e.g. To mask Co, Cu thioacetanide or sodium sulphide is used, to damask them dimercaprol is used.

6. Titrations with instrumental detection

Simple, back as well as replacement titrations, where suitable indicator is not available, instrumental detection like spectrophotometry, potentiometry, coulometry or amperometry can be used.

In electroanalytical methods, mercury indicator electrode is used.

7. Miscellaneous titrations [Indirect determinations]

(a) Fluorides are not directly titrable with EDTA so, they are first precipitated as lead fluoride, the precipitate thus formed is dissolved in dil. HNO_3, titrate liberated Pb^{2+} lead with EDTA using xylenol orange indicator.

(b) Ag/Au also cannot be directly titrated, hence they are exchanged with Ni ions from tetracyanonickel ions; liberated Ni is titrated with EDTA.

$$2Ag^+ + [Ni(CN)_4]^{2-} \rightleftharpoons 2[Ag(CN)_2]^- + Ni^{2+}$$

Mixture Analysis

Selectivity in complexometric titrations

Disodium EDTA is widely used in complexometry because it has ability to form stable complexes with number of metals. However, it is disadvantageous in following cases.

(i) Analysis of mixtures.

(ii) Analysis of metals in presence of other metallic impurities.

So in order to achieve selectivity in titration, following approaches can be used.

1. Masking and demasking

Masking: It is the process/technique of adding a component to the solution that complexes strongly with one of the metals, thus decreasing its conditional constant with EDTA so that this metal is not titrable, then the second metal is available for titration without interference. Reagent is called as masking agent.

Masking can be achieved by following means.

(a) Precipitation

This is formation of insoluble complex with metal interfering in titration.

Table 6.2: Masking Agents and the metals they precipitate

Reagent/Masking agent	Metals
Thioacetamide	Co^{2+}, Cu^{2+}, Pb^{2+}
Sodium sulphide	Co^{2+}, Cu^{2+}, Pb^{2+}
Sulphate	Pb^{2+}, Ba^{2+}
Oxalate	Ca^{2+}, Pb^{2+}
Fluoride	Ca^{2+}, Mg^{2+}, Pb^{2+}
Ferrocyanide	Zn^{2+}, Cu^{2+}
Dimercaprol	Mg^{2+}, Cd^{2+}, Zn^{2+}, As^{2+}, Tn^{2+}, Pb^{2+}, Bi^{3+}

(b) pH control

Alkaline earth metals form complex with edetate below pH 7, hence pH must be maintained above 7 if they interfere. Transition elements form complexes at pH below 3 and tin, iron, Co, thorium form at still low pH. So pH should be controlled so that interfering metals does not form complex with EDTA.

(c) Complexation

Ammonium fluoride forms soluble complexes with Al, iron, Ti and thus mask them. Cyanide forms complex with Cd, Zn, Hg^{2+}, Cu, Co, Ni, Ag, Pt but not with Mg and Pb.

(d) Reduction and complexation

Those metals which cannot be masked directly can be reduced first and then complexed.

e.g. $$Fe^{3+} \xrightarrow{\text{Reduction}} Fe^{2+}$$

Fe^{2+} can now form complex with hexacyanoferrate which is stable and less intense in colour than Fe^{3+} complex.

(e) Kinetic masking

If interfering metals or metals in mixture have different [slow] rate of complex formation with EDTA e.g. Fe^{3+}, Cr^{3+}, they can be prevented from reaction by performing rapid titration or boiling and further cooling the solution.

Generally, in such cases, cold solution of EDTA is added; solution is boiled, cooled and titrated against lead nitrate.

Demasking

Masking is a process in which a substance without physical separation of it or its reaction products, is so transformed that it does not enter into a particular reaction.

Demasking is the process in which the masked substance regains its ability to enter in a particular reaction.

There are several examples of demasking.

1. Dimercaprol can displace Co^{2+}, Cu^{2+} from their complex.

2. Zn^{2+}, Cd^{2+}, Cu^{2+} masked with KCN, can be demasked with aldehydes or chloral hydrate or methanol-ethanoic acid solution.

$$[Zn\ (CN)_4]^{2-} + 4H^+ + 4HCO \rightarrow Zn^{2+} + 4HO \cdot CH_2 \cdot CN$$

Demasked

Examples of Masking and Demasking

Mixture: Mg^{2+}, Zn^{2+}, Cu^{2+}

Step 1. Add excess of EDTA, it will react with all three metals, back titrate excess of titrant with standard Mg solution. This gives concentration of all three.

Step 2. To another sample add excess as KCN, it will mask Zn^{2+} and Cu^{2+}. Titrate with EDTA, it gives amount of Mg^{2+}. To the same solution add chloral hydrate or methanol : ethanoic acid (3 : 1), this damasks Zn^{2+} and titration with EDTA gives content of Zn^{2+}.

Step 3. Subtract content of Mg^{2+} and Zn^{2+} from total content to obtain content of Cu^{2+}.

Other methods to achieve selectivity in complexomctry.

2. **Classical separation:** Allow interfering metal to form precipitate, filter to separate. Re dissolve the precipitate to obtain content of metal that has precipitated.

3. **Solvent extraction:** From mixture of Zn, Cu and Pb, the Zn can be separated by adding excess of ammonium thiocyanate and extracting Zn thiocyanate with 4-methylpentan-2-one, dilute with water and determine content of Zn.

4. **Use of ion exchange resins:** Anions like phosphate can be removed by extraction with ion exchange resins.

6.7 TITRATION CURVE

As with other types of titrations, when $-\log$ of concentration of metal ion [pM] is plotted vs. volume of titrant, a sigmoidal curve is obtained.

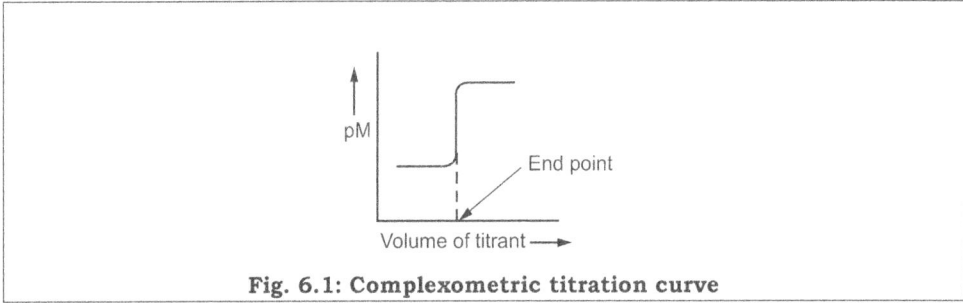

Fig. 6.1: Complexometric titration curve

Pharmacopoeial assays by complexometry

- Assay of Ca gluconate injection.

- Assay of $CaCl_2$ in compound sodium chloride injection (ringers injection).

- Assay of magnesium sulphate.

6.8 DISODIUM EDTA

- Disodium EDTA is salt of ethylene diamine tetra acetic acid.

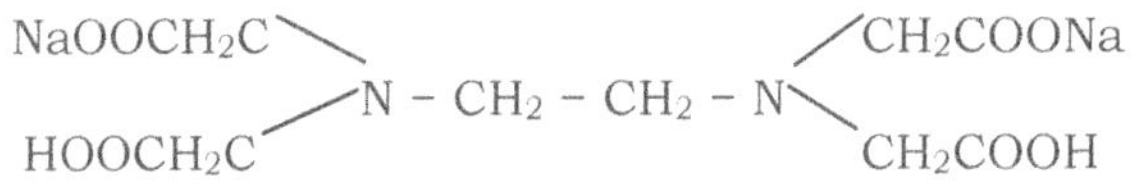

$$NaOOCH_2C \diagdown \atop HOOCH_2C \diagup N - CH_2 - CH_2 - N \diagup CH_2COONa \atop \diagdown CH_2COOH$$

- It is the most popular complexing agent used in complexometry. It is denoted as Y. EDTA is not soluble in water hence its disodium salt is used.

- It has amino and carboxylic acid groups to complex with metal. Particularly, 'N' and 'O' atoms form co-ordinate bonds with metal.

- Thus, EDTA has number of sites to form bonds with metal.

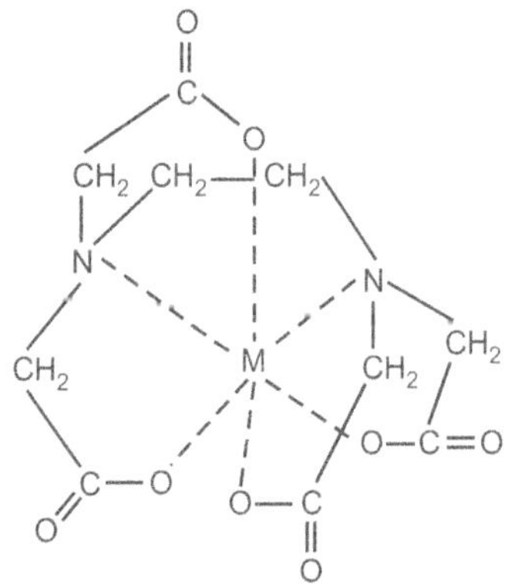

Fig. 6.2: Metal complex with EDTA

Preparation and standerdisation of 0.1 M Disodium EDTA solution as per IP 2014

Dissolve 37.2g of disodium edetate in sufficient water to produce 1000 ml.

Standardisation

Weigh accurately about 0.8 g of granulated zinc, dissolve by gently warming in 12 ml of dil. HCl and 0.1 ml of bromine water. Boil to remove excess bromine and cool and add sufficient water to make 200 ml of solution. Pipette 20 ml of resulting solution in a flask and neutralise with 2M NaOH. Dilute to about 150 ml with water, add sufficient ammonia buffer pH 10, to dissolve the precipitate and add 5 ml in excess.

Add 50 mg of mordant black II mixture and titrate with the disodium edetate solution until the solution turns green.

1 ml of 0.1 M disodium edetate $\cong$ 0.000654 g of Zn.

Have you heard about him?

Alfred Werner (12 December 1866-15 November 1919) was a Swiss chemist who won the Nobel Prize in Chemistry in 1913 in recognition of his work on atomic bonding in molecules, for proposing the octahedral configuration of transition metal complexes which shed new light onto earlier studies and opened up new research fields, especially in inorganic chemistry.

Werner developed the basis for modern coordination chemistry. He was the first inorganic chemist to win the Nobel Prize, and the only one prior to 1973. Werner discarded Kekule's distinction between "valence" compounds, which are eminently explainable using classical valence theory, and "molecular compounds", which are not. Werner proposed a new approach in which the configurations of some compounds metal-ammines ("Werner complexes"), double salts, and metal salt hydrates – were logical consequences of their coordination numbers (a new concept) and two types of valence, primary and secondary.

7

OXIDATION-REDUCTION REACTIONS AND TITRATION

7.1 THEORY AND HALF REACTIONS

Redox is the abbreviation of 'Reduction-oxidation' system. In reduction-oxidation methods of analysis, electron transfer occurs from one species to another and the electrical potential of this electron transfer is measured. This electric potential also suggests the tendency of a reaction to occur.

When quantity of pure component is estimated based on the measurement of volume of the standard solution that reacts completely with analyte then such oxidation-reduction reaction method is called as redox titration.

This is the titration where 'change is valency of reacting species' takes place. This is in contrast with precipitation and neutralisation methods where no change in valency occurs.

$$\text{Valency} = \text{Number of electrons released/taken by the reacting species}$$

This valency also depends on the compound in which the element is present. e.g. $FeCl_2$ - Iron has valency of 2. $FeCl_3$ - Iron has valency of 3.

Thus, redox reaction is transfer of electrons from one species to another resulting in change of valency of reacting species.

$$FeCl_3 + e^- \xrightarrow{\text{Reduction}} FeCl_2$$

$$\text{Valency '+3'} \qquad\qquad \text{Valency '+2'}$$

Oxidation: It is the process which involves either of the following-

(i)   Addition of oxygen

e.g. $SO_2 + O \rightarrow SO_3$

(ii)   Loss of hydrogen

e.g. $H_2S + O \rightarrow S + H_2O$

(iii) Loss of electrons

e.g. $Sn^{2+} \rightarrow Sn^{4+}$, $Fe^{2+} \rightarrow Fe^{3+}$

Reduction: It involves either of the following-

(i)   Addition of hydrogen

e.g. $C_2H_4 + 2H^+ \rightarrow C_2H_6$

(ii)   Loss of oxygen

e.g. $CuO + 2H^+ \rightarrow Cu + H_2O$

(iii) Gain of electrons

e.g. $Sn^{4+} \rightarrow Sn^{2+}$, $Fe^{3+} \rightarrow Fe^{2+}$

Oxidising agents: These are the agents which oxidise others and themselves get reduced. e.g. Potassium permanganate ($KMnO_4$), Iodine(I_2)

Reducing agents: These are the agents which reduce others and themselves get oxidised. e.g. Titanous trichoride ($TiCl_3$), Sodium thiosulphate ($Na_2S_2O_3$), Potassium iodide (KI).

Half reactions

•   Reaction explaining change in oxidation state (degree of oxidation of an atom in chemical compound) of an individual substance is called as half reaction.

- It can be either oxidation or reduction.
- Half reaction is often used to describe reaction occurring at each electrode in an electrochemical cell.
- Half reactions are also used to balance redox reactions.
- Two half reactions [oxidation and reduction] make one complete redox reaction upon balancing them.

    e.g. Oxidation of ferrous to ferric

$$Fe^{2+} \rightarrow Fe^{3+} + e^-$$

Reduction of cerric to cerrous

$$Ce^{++} + e^- \rightarrow Ce^{3+}$$

Complete redox reaction

$$Fe^{2+} + Ce^{4+} \rightarrow Fe^{3+} + Ce^{3+}$$

Methods for calculation of equivalent weight of redox substance.

1. Oxidation number method
2. Half reaction/ion electron method.

By both the methods the number of electrons transferred during a reaction is calculated. Molecular weight is divided by the number of electrons to get the equivalent weight.

$$\text{Equivalence weight} = \frac{\text{Molecular weight}}{\text{Valency}}$$

$\therefore \qquad \text{Equivalent Weight} = \dfrac{\text{Molecular weight}}{\text{Number of electrons}}$

1. Equivalent weight of iodine

$$I_2 + 2e^- \rightleftharpoons 2I^-$$

2 electrons are transferred; so equivalent weight of iodine $= \dfrac{\text{Molecular weight}}{2}$

2. Equivalent weight of arsenic trioxide

$$As_2O_3 + 3H_2O \rightarrow 2H_3AsO_3$$

$$2H_3AsO_3 + 2H_2O \rightarrow 2H_3AsO_4 + 4H^+ + 4e^-$$

So, $\qquad \text{Equivalent weight} = \dfrac{\text{Molecular weight}}{4}$

We have four in the denominator because four electrons are lost in the reaction.

3. Sodium oxalate

$$Na_2C_2O_4 \rightarrow Na^{2+} + C_2O_4^{2-}$$

$$C_2O_4^{2-} + 2H^+ \rightarrow 2CO_2 + 2H^+ + 2e^-$$

$$\text{Equivalent weight} = \frac{\text{Molecular weight}}{2}$$

4. Cerric ammonium sulphate

$$Ce^{4+} + e^- \rightleftharpoons Ce^{3+}$$

$$\text{Equivalent weight} = \frac{\text{Molecular weight}}{1}$$

5. Sodium thiosulfate

$$2S_2O_3^{2-} \rightleftharpoons S_4O_6^{2-} + 2e^-$$

$$\text{Equivalent weight} = \frac{\text{Molecular weight}}{2}$$

6. Oxalic acid

$$C_2O_4^{2-} \rightleftharpoons 2CO_2 + 2e^-$$

$$\text{Equivalent weight} = \frac{\text{Molecular weight}}{2}$$

7. Potassium iodate (acidic pH)

$$IO_3^- + 6H^+ + 6e^- \rightleftharpoons I^- + 3H_2O$$

$$\text{Equivalent weight} = \frac{\text{Molecular weight}}{6}$$

8. Titanous trichloride

$$Ti^{3+} \rightleftharpoons Ti^{4+} + e^-$$

$$\text{Equivalent weight} = \frac{\text{Molecular weight}}{1}$$

9. KMnO$_4$ at acidic pH:

$$MnO_4^- + 8H^+ + 5e^- \rightleftharpoons Mn^{2+} + 4H_2O$$

$$\text{Equivalent weight} = \frac{\text{Molecular weight}}{5}$$

KMnO$_4$ at basic pH

$$MnO_4 + e^- \rightleftharpoons MnO_4^{2-}$$

$$\text{Equivalent weight} = \frac{\text{Molecular weight}}{1}$$

KMnO$_4$ at neutral pH

$$MnO_4^- + 2H_2O + 3e^- \rightleftharpoons MnO_2 + 4OH^-$$

$$\text{Equivalent weight} = \frac{\text{Molecular weight}}{2}$$

Give reasons

1. H$_2$SO$_4$ is used in redox titration.

Acidification is sometimes needed in redox titrations. For acidification, H$_2$SO$_4$ is used/preferred over HNO$_3$ or HCl. It is because HCl [potential + 1.36 V] is a reducing agent and HNO$_3$ [potential + 0.96 V] is an oxidising agent. However, H$_2$SO$_4$ is an indifferent acid as it does not undergo oxidation or reduction.

7.2 NERNST EQUATION

- In a redox reaction, energy released in a reaction due to movement of charged particles gives rise to a potential difference (electromotive force).

- It is an equation used widely to determine cell potential at any moment during a reaction under non-standard conditions.

$$E_{cell} = E_{cell}^{o} - \frac{RT}{nF} \ln Q \qquad \text{For total cell}$$

$$E_{red} = E_{red}^{o} + \frac{RT}{nF} \ln \frac{a_{ox}}{a_{Red}} \qquad \text{Half cell potential for reduction}$$

E^{o} = Standard potential

R = Universal gas constant 8.314 JK^{-1} mol^{-1}

T = Absolute temperature

n = Number of electrons

F = Faraday constant = 9.648×10^{4} C mol^{-1}

Q = Reaction quotient

A = Activity of oxidant and reductant

E_{cell} = Cell potential

E_{red} = Reduction potential

- Nernst equation at 25°C or 298 K and converting natural log to log to the base 10 becomes

$$E \qquad \qquad = E^{o} - \frac{0.059}{n} \log Q$$

- It means half cell potential will change by 59 mV when concentration involved in one electron oxidation or reduction will change 10 fold.

- It is applicable only in dilute ionic solutions containing concentration less than 10^{-3} M.

7.3 METHODS TO BALANCE REDOX REACTIONS

1. **Oxidation number (oxidation state) method/Electron balance method-Oxidation number:** Residual charge which atom appears to have/has when all other atoms from the molecule are removed as ions.

Atoms can have positive, zero or negative oxidation numbers depending upon their state of combination.

Rules

1. Oxidation number of element in free state is always zero.

    e.g. He, Cl_2, H_2, $O_2 = 0$.

2. Oxidation number of any simple one atom ion is equal to its charge.

    e.g. $Na^+ = +1$, $Ca^{2+} = +2$, $Cl^- = -1$.

3. Oxidation number of oxygen is '–2' in all compounds except in peroxides.

    e.g. H_2O, H_2SO_4, NO_2, CO_2. $= -2$

4. Oxidation number of hydrogen in any non-ionic compounds is +1 except metal hydrides [NaH] it is –1.

5. The algebraic sum of oxidation numbers of all atoms in the formula for a neutral compound is zero. In combinations of non-metal not involving 'H' or 'O', the non-metal which is more electronegative will have oxidation number equal to its charge on its most commonly encountered negative ion.

e.g. CCl_4	Cl $_{-1}$	C $_{+4}$		PO_4^{3-}	P $_{+5}$	O $_{-2}$
CH_4	H $_{+1}$	C $_{-4}$		SO_4^{2-}	O $_{-2}$	S $_{+6}$
SF_6	F $_{-1}$	S $_{+6}$		NF_3	F $_{-1}$	N $_{+3}$
CS_2	S $_{-2}$	C $_{+4}$		MOO_4^{2-}	O $_{-2}$	MO $_{+6}$
NH_4Cl	Cl $_{-1}$	H $_{+1}$ N $_{-3}$		CO_2	O $_{-2}$	C $_{+4}$
NH_4^+	H $_{+1}$	N $_{-3}$		$Cr_2O_7^{2-}$	O $_{-2}$	Cr $_{+6}$

6. In a chemical reaction, the total oxidation number is conserved. If the oxidation number of an atom increases during a chemical reaction, that reaction is oxidation. If the oxidation number of an atom decreases during a chemical reaction, that reaction is reduction.

Balancing by Oxidation Number Method

$$MnO_2 + Cl^- \rightarrow Mn^{2+} + Cl_2 + H_2O$$

Step 1: Write the skeleton equation and indicate oxidation number of each element and identify elements undergoing change in oxidation number.

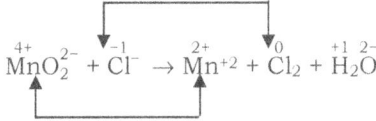

Increases by 1

Oxidation [loss of 1 electron]

$$\overset{4+}{MnO_2^{2-}} + \overset{-1}{Cl^-} \rightarrow \overset{2+}{Mn^{+2}} + \overset{0}{Cl_2} + \overset{+1\ 2-}{H_2O}$$

Decrease by 2
Reduction [gain of 2 electrons]

Step 2: Equalise the increase/decrease in oxidation number on reactant side by multiplying the respective formulae with suitable integers.

(Multiply MnO_2 by 1 and Cl^- by 2).

$$MnO_2 + 2Cl^- \rightarrow Mn^{2+} + Cl_2 + H_2O$$

Step 3: Balance all other atoms except H and O.

Step 3: Balance for O atoms by adding H_2O and then by hydrogen.

$$4H^+ + MnO_2 + 2Cl^- \rightarrow Mn^{2+} + Cl_2 + 2H_2O$$

Oxidation number method can be used to determine equivalent weight of substances

$$Equivalent\ weight = \frac{Molecular\ weight}{Increase\ or\ decrease\ in\ oxidation\ number}$$

e.g. KMnO₄

At alkaline pH $MnO_4^- \rightarrow MnO_4^{2-}$

$\underset{7+}{}{}^{2-} \qquad \underset{6+}{}{}^{2-} \qquad 7 \longrightarrow 6 = 1$

At neutral pH

$MnO_4^- \rightarrow MnO_2$

$\underset{7+}{}{}^{2-} \qquad \underset{4+}{}{}^{2-} \qquad 7 \longrightarrow 4 = 3$

At acidic pH

$MnO_4^- \rightarrow Mn^{2+}$

$\underset{7+}{}{}^{2-} \qquad {}_{2+} \qquad 7 \longrightarrow 2 = 5$

2. **Half reaction method [Ion-electron method]**

$$KMnO_4 + H_2SO_4 + FeSO_4 \rightarrow Fe(SO_4)_3 + K_2SO_4 + 2MnSO_4 + H_2O$$

Step 1: Write half reactions

$$MnO_4^- \rightarrow Mn^{+2} \qquad Fe^{2+} \rightarrow Fe^{3+}$$

Step 2: Balance oxygens, hydrogens and then electrons.

(a) $8H^+ + MnO_4^- + 5e^- \xrightarrow[\text{Gain (Reduction)}]{} Mn^{2+} + 4H_2O$ $5e^-$

(b) $Fe^{2+} \xrightarrow[\text{Oxidation}]{\text{Loss}} Fe^{3+} + e^-$ $1e^-$

Step 3: Multiply oxidation reaction by 5 [because 5 electrons are gained in reduction].

$$5Fe^{2+} \rightarrow 5Fe^{3+} + 5e^-$$

$$8H^+ + MnO_4^- + 5e^- \rightarrow Mn^{2+} + 4H_2O$$

Overall reaction by cancelling 5e⁻ from both the reactions

$$MnO_4^- + 8H^+ + 5Fe^{2+} \rightarrow 5Fe^{3+} + Mn^{2+} + 4H_2O$$

Complete reaction-

$$2KMnO_4 + 8H_2SO_4 + 10FeSO_4 \rightarrow 5Fe_2(SO_4)_3 + 2MnSO_4 + K_2SO_4 + 8H_2O$$

$$\text{Equivalent weight} = \frac{\text{Molecular weight}}{\text{Number of electrons}} \text{ [Here for KMnO}_4 \text{ it is 5]}$$

7.4 REDOX TITRATION CURVE

Redox titration involves oxidation and reduction of two substances simultaneously. One substance is taken as analyte and another substance is taken as titrant. As titration proceeds, redox potential is monitored with the help of electrodes. This potential is measured after each 1 ml or 0.5 ml addition of titrant and is plotted against volume of titrant added. This plot is called as redox titration curve.

Potential rises gradually before and after end point of titration and curve is sigmoidal in shape.

e.g. Reaction of ferrous and cerric salts.

$$Fe^{2+} + Ce^{4+} \rightarrow Fe^{3+} + Ce^{3+}$$

Ferrous Cerric   Ferric Cerrous

Half reaction 1

$$Fe^{2+} \xrightarrow{\text{Oxidation}} Fe^{3+}$$

Ferrous   Ferric

Half reaction 2

Reduction

$$Ce^{4+} \rightarrow Ce^{3+}$$

Cerric   Cerrous

Redox potential

$$E_{ox/red} = E° - \frac{RT}{nF} \ln \frac{[Red]}{[OX]}$$

So for half reaction 1

$$E_{Fe^{3+}/Fe^{2+}} = +0.767 - \frac{RT}{nF} \ln \frac{[Fe^{2+}]}{[Fe^{3+}]} \qquad \text{... (1)}$$

For half reaction 2

$$E_{Ce^{4+}/Ce^{3+}} = +1.70 - \frac{RT}{nF} \ln \frac{[Ce^{3+}]}{[Ce^{4+}]} \qquad \text{... (2)}$$

$$E_{total} = \frac{0.767 + 1.70}{2} - \frac{RT}{nF} \frac{[Fe^{2+}]\,[Ce^{3+}]}{[Fe^{3+}]\,[Ce^{4+}]} \qquad \text{... (3)}$$

$$\text{Concentration of any ion} = \frac{\text{Molarity} \times \text{Volume}}{\text{Total volume}}$$

Suppose 50 ml of 0.1 M ferrous salt is taken in a flask and 0.1 M cerric salt is taken in a burette.

1. Before addition of titrant

$$[Fe^{2+}] = \frac{0.1 \times 50}{50} = 0.1$$

2. After addition of 5 ml of titrant

$$[Fe^{2+}] = \frac{\text{Initial} - \text{Reacted}}{55}$$

$$= \frac{0.1 \times 50 - 0.1 \times 5}{55}$$

$$= 0.081$$

$$[Fe^{3+}] = \frac{0.1 \times 5}{55} = 0.009$$

3. After addition of exact 50 ml of titrant i.e. at the end point.

$$E = +1.23 \text{ V}$$

It is calculated by equation 3.

4. After adding excess of titrant i.e. 60 ml

$$[Ce^{3+}] = \frac{\text{Concentration of } Fe^{2+}}{110} = \frac{0.1 \times 50}{110} = 0.045$$

$$[Ce^{4+}] = \frac{\text{Concentration added} - \text{Reacted}}{110}$$

$$= \frac{0.1 \times 60 - 0.1 \times 50}{110}$$

$$= 0.009$$

$$E = +1.66 \text{ V}$$

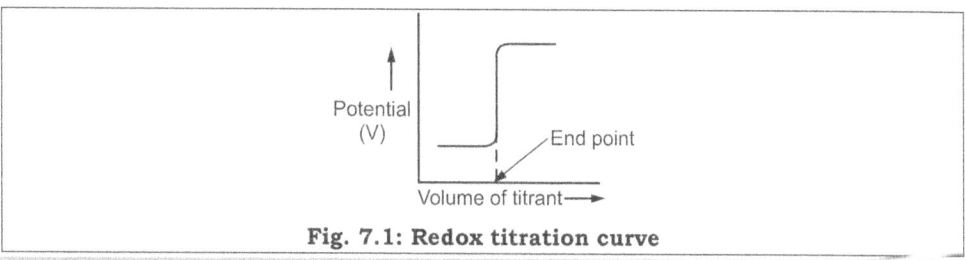

Fig. 7.1: Redox titration curve

7.5 REDOX INDICATORS

End point detection in Redox Titration

It is the point at which oxidation/reduction is complete, extra drops of titrant do not undergo reaction with analyte. As there is no further reaction, there is sudden change in electric potential at the end point.

Location of end point can be achieved by –

(i)   Measurement of electric potential directly by 'potentiometry'.

(ii)   Visual observation of colour change by using 'self indicator' titrants.

(iii) Addition of reagents capable of showing colour change in their oxidised/ reduced form i.e. 'Internal/External' indicators.

1.   Potentiometry

This is an instrumental method where there is continuous monitoring of electric potential. At the start of the reaction there is sharp fall/rise in potential which changes suddenly/abruptly at the end point giving inflection in the titration curve.

Instrument consists of a reaction vessel in which two electrodes (Indicator and Reference) are immersed. Titrant is allowed to fall from burette to a stirred solution of analyte **(Fig. 7.2)**.

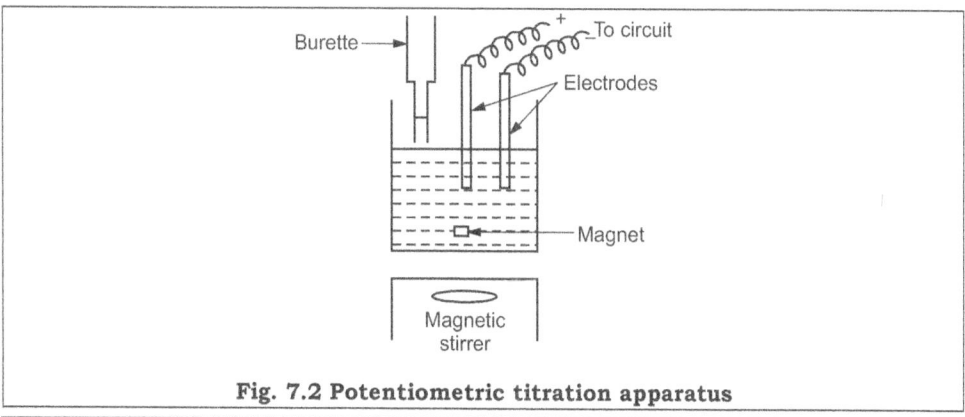

Fig. 7.2 Potentiometric titration apparatus

Potential (E) is plotted against volume of titrant resulting in a sigmoidal curve **(Fig. 7.3)** Inflection in curve describes the end point. Sometimes the first derivative $\Delta E/\Delta V$ is plotted, where end point is the peak maxima **(Fig. 7.4)**.

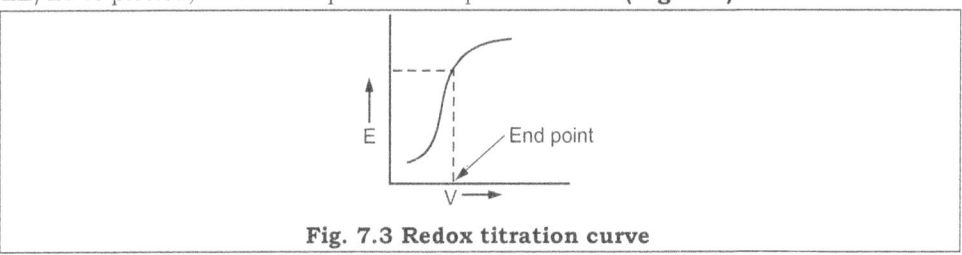

Fig. 7.3 Redox titration curve

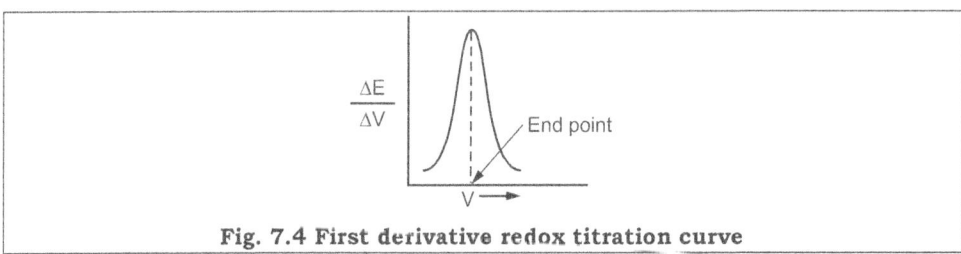

Fig. 7.4 First derivative redox titration curve

Advantages

1. It can be applied to coloured solutions.
2. It can be applied to very dilute solutions.
3. It can be used where visual detection is not possible e.g. turbid solutions.
4. Redox as well as neutralisation, precipitation, complexometric titrations can be performed.

Limitations

1. Instrumental method, so needs power supply.
2. Calibration of instrument is necessary.
3. Time consuming, as it involves measurement of potential after each 0.5 ml/1 ml addition of titrant.

Example: Assay of hydralazine HCl as per IP 2014

Titrant: 0.05 M Potassium iodate.

Reference electrode - Calomel. Indicator electrode - Platinum

2. Self indicators

If the titrant used in reaction has different colours in its oxidised and reduced electronic states, they themselves can be used as indicators; these are known as self indicators.

$KMnO_4$ has pink colour in its oxidised state. It is an oxidising agent, so when it reacts with the analyte it undergoes reduction [Mn^{2+}, MnO_2] to form colourless manganous ions. After completion of reaction, extra drop of $KMnO_4$ remains pink in colour as there is no analyte which can reduce it.

$$MnO_4^- \xrightarrow{\text{Reduction}} Mn^{+2}$$

Pink   Colourless

Cerric ammonium sulphate is 'yellow' in its oxidised state, which eventually fades to give colourless cerrous ions on reduction, but colour change from 'faint yellow → colourless' is not so marked as it is for $KMnO_4$. Same is the case with iodine.

Standard redox potential (mv)for $KMnO_4$ reactions is

$$\left.\begin{array}{l} MnO_4^- \rightarrow MnO_2 + 1.59 \\ MnO_4^- \rightarrow Mn^{2+} + 1.52 \end{array}\right\} \text{Platinum electrodes}$$

Advantages

1. As titrant itself shows colour change, no need of the addition of any other indicator.

2. Detection of visual end point is possible, no need of instrumental detection.

Limitations

1. $KMnO_4$ is the only titrant which shows marked difference in colour, so cannot be applied to all other types of redox titrations [cerimetry, iodometry, iodimetry].

2. It leads to slight over titration.

    Example: Assay of H_2O_2 solution as per IP 2014

    Titrant: $KMnO_4$.

3. Internal indicators

These are indicators which show different colour in their oxidised and reduced form. Their redox potential should be between titrant and analyte to show sharp, readily detectable colour change.

$$In_{oxi} + ne \rightleftharpoons In_{red}$$

Ferroin [Ortho 1, 10 phenanthroline ferrous ion] has intense red colour and shows pale blue colour as it undergoes oxidation.

$$[Fe(C_{12}H_8N_2)_3]^{+++} + e^- \rightleftharpoons [Fe(C_{12}H_8N_2)_3]^{++}$$

Pale blue (oxidised)   Deep red (reduced)

Standard redox potential is 1.14 volts.

Other reagents

Name	Oxidised form	Reduced form	Standard potential (V)
1. Methylene blue	Blue	Colourless	0.52
2. Diphenylamine	Violet	Colourless	0.76
3. Ferroin	Blue	Red	1.14

Diphenyl amine

Colourless   Diphenyl amine   Violet $+2H^+ + 2e^-$

These indicators are added to the analyte solution and as they are capable of undergoing redox reaction, extra drop of titrant after end point oxidises or reduces indicator giving the colour change.

Advantages

1. Variety of indicators are available with a wide range of their standard electrical potentials.

2. Sharp end points are obtained.

Limitations

1. Usually fresh indicators need to be prepared every time.

2. Potential of indicator reaction should match the redox reaction involved in titration.

Example: Assay of ascorbic acid tablets as per IP 2014

Titrant: Cerric ammonium sulphate.

Indicator: Ferroin sulphate.

Ferroin solution: 0.7 g of ferrous sulfate + 1.5g of 1, 10 phenanthroline HCl in 70 ml water, add sufficient water to produce 100 ml.

Oxidised form
pale Blue

Reduced form
Red

Structure of ferroin

Internal indicators added towards end point of titration

For titrations involving iodine as titrant, starch solution is used as the indicator. Iodine has yellow to brown colour which is turns colourless on reduction. Locating end point from yellow to colourless is difficult, so starch can be used in such titrations.

Starch reacts with iodine to form intense blue coloured complex, which is visible at very low concentrations of iodine.

Advantages

1. Great sensitivity, visible blue colour when iodide is greater than 4×10^{-4} M and iodine greater than 2×10^{-5} M.

2. Starch is inexpensive.

Limitations

1. It has to be added towards end point of titration.

2. Starch is insoluble in cold water, so suspension is prepared in hot water, which is not very stable.

3. Sometimes drift in endpoint is seen particularly in dilute solutions.

Sodium starch glycollate overcomes limitations of starch. It gives stable solutions and can be added at any stage of the titration.

4. External indicators

Here, near the equivalence point, a drop of reaction mixture is removed with a glass rod and placed on drop/strip of indicator. Colour change is observed outside the reaction vessel.

Example: When ferrous ions are titrated against potassium dichromate, a drop of solution is brought in contact with potassium ferricyanide and failure to give blue colour is observed as the end point. Starch iodide paste in sodium nitrite solution is also an example of an external indicator.

Advantage

1. When indicator is not suitable/stable in the solution, this method is used.

Limitations

1. Observation of spontaneous colour change is important because air oxidation can also lead to colour formation slowly.

2. Loss of reaction mixture takes place, which is contrary to principle of volumetric titrations.

$$KI + HCl \rightarrow HI + KCl$$

$$2HI + 2HNO_2 \rightarrow I_2\uparrow + 2NO + 2H_2O$$

$$\downarrow$$

Starch

(Blue colour)

7.6 PERMANGANATE TITRATIONS

Potassium permanganate ($KMnO_4$) is a widely used titrant in redox titrations. It is a strong oxidising agent mostly used under acidic conditions. As it gives manganous ions which are colourless and $KMnO_4$ is intense pink in colour, it acts as a self indicator.

$$MnO_4^{2-} + 8H^+ + 5e^- \rightleftharpoons Mn^{2+} + 4H_2O$$

*   Maximum stability of $KMnO_4$ is in neutral condition.

    At acidic pH it forms manganous ions which react with $KMnO_4$ to form MnO_2.

    At alkaline pH it forms MnO_4^{2-} which accelerate decomposition of $KMnO_4$ to form more MnO_2 to promote the rate of decomposition. So, in acid/alkali progressive decrease in strength of $KMnO_4$ occurs.

* $KMnO_4$ is not available as primary standard grade so must be standardised using reducing agents. e.g. As_2O_3 [acidic/basic solutions of arsenious oxide are not stable; hence use neutral pH].   Oxidation of As_2O_3 is not rapid at R.T. It is quick and possible at RT in presence of iodine, iodate or iodine monochloride as catalysts. End point is colourless → Pink when $KMnO_4$ is used as self indicator. With ferroin [o-phenanthroline - ferrous sulphate] as indicator the end point is Pink → Blue. $KMnO_4$ can be used in the assay of As_2O_3.

*   When iodine is titrated with $KMnO_4$, as both solutions are highly coloured, HCN is added which forms ICN and which is colourless.

$$I^- + HCN \rightleftharpoons ICN + H^+ + 2e$$

End point can be determined by adding ferroin; also this can be used for standardisation of KMnO₄.

- It can also be standardised by Na oxalate, oxalic acid.

$$C_2O_4^{2-} + 2H^+ \rightleftharpoons H_2C_2O_4$$

$$H_2C_2O_4 \rightarrow 2CO_2 + 2H^+ + 2e$$

- Reaction is slow, catalysed by manganous ions and can be carried out at elevated temperatures for rapid reaction to occur and for accurate location of end point. Any metal that can form insoluble oxalate [Ca^{2+}, Ba^{2+}, Pb^{2+}, Ag^+, Mg^{2+}, Zn^{2+}] can be determined by forming insoluble oxalate with oxalic acid, dissolving precipitate

  in dil. H_2SO_4 and titrating the liberated oxalic acid with permanganate.

- Ferrous is oxidised to ferric and can be determined by KMnO₄, but ferric sulfate is yellow in colour and it converts the pink colour of permanganate to orange. Phosphoric acid can be added which forms a colourless complex with ferric ion.

- If ferrous is titrated against KMnO₄ in presence of Cl⁻ ions, Cl⁻ ions consume some KMnO₄ and correct estimation of ferrous is not possible. This problem can be overcome by adding manganous ions or Reinhardt-Zimmermann solution [RZ]. RZ solution contains $MgSO_4$, phosphoric acid and H_2SO_4.

- Determination of chlorate, perchlorate, nitrate, vanadium, chromium is possible indirectly.

- Assay of permanganate itself can be done by titration against ferrous ions, which oxidises to ferric ions. If ferrous form is not available, ferric ions are first reduced to ferrous [using Jones reductor (amalgamated zinc)] and then reacted with KMnO₄.

Preparation and standardisation of KMnO₄ as per Indian Pharmacopoeia

Preparation 0.02 M KMnO₄

- Dissolve 3.2 g of KMnO₄ in 1000 ml of water, heat on a water bath for 1 hour, allow to stand for 2 days and filter through glass wool.

Problems

1. KMnO₄ often contains small proportion of MnO_2 [reduced form of KMnO₄].

2. Equivalent weight of KMnO₄ is different in all pH conditions [acidic, basic and neutral]. Hence, normal and molar solutions are not always the same.

3. Intense colour of the solution makes detection of undissolved solid difficult.

- Heating is suggested for oxidation of all oxidisable impurities in water and filteration for their removal. Filtration also removes precipitate of MnO_2 which is formed by reduction of $KMnO_4$ itself at neutral pH.

- It mostly oxidises Cl^- which may be present in water. Aqueous solutions of $KMnO_4$ are not stable, it readily decomposes on exposure to light, heat, acid or base to Mn^{2+} and MnO_4. Hence, they should be prepared fresh and stored at neutral pH.

$$MnO_4^- \xrightarrow{\text{Alkali}} MnO_4^{2-}$$

$$MnO_4^- \xrightarrow{\text{Acid}} Mn^{2+}$$

Alternative procedure

Weigh accurately 3.2 g of $KMnO_4$ on a watch glass, transfer to a beaker containing cold water, stir to break the crystals with a glass rod. Decant into graduated flask leaving undissolved residues in the beaker. Add more water to the beaker and repeat until all $KMnO_4$ dissolves. Make up the volume to one litre with water.

Storage

Great care must be taken while handling $KMnO_4$ as dangerous explosions are liable to occur if it is brought into contact with organic or other readily oxidisable substances, either in solution or under dry condition.

Standardisation as per IP 2014

- To 25 ml of solution of 0.02 M $KMnO_4$ in a glass-stoppered flask, add 2g of potassium iodide, followed by 10 ml of 1M H_2SO_4. Titrate liberated iodine with 0.1M $Na_2S_2O_3$ using 3 ml of starch solution, added to towards the end of the titration, as indicator. Perform blank and make necessary correction.

    1 ml of 0.1M $Na_2S_2O_3 \cong 0.00316$ g of $KMnO_4$

Store protected from light.

Alternative procedures for standardisation

1. **By use of oxalic acid/Na oxalate**

    Na oxalate is preferred because of it availability in pure form; oxalic acid is available in dehydrate form.

    $2KMnO_4 + 5H_2C_2O_4 + 3H_2SO_4 \rightarrow K_2SO_4 + 2MnSO_4 + 10CO_2 + 5H_2O$

    Reduction $MnO_4^- \rightarrow Mn^{2+}$

    Oxidation $C_2O_4^- \rightarrow 2CO_2$

Also oxalic acid is hygroscopic and looses its water on standing. Na oxalate is not hygroscopic.

$$2KMnO_4 + 5Na_2C_2O_4 + 5H_2SO_4 \rightarrow K_2SO_4 + 2MnSO_4 + 10CO_2 + 5Na_2SO_4 + 8H_2O$$

Weigh accurately 0.3g Na oxalate/equivalent oxalic acid, mix with 30 ml dil. H_2SO_4 and heat at 70-80°C, titrate against 0.1N $KMnO_4$ till faint pink colour persists.

2.   By use of arsenic trioxide

Weigh accurately 0.25g As_2O_3, add 10 ml NaOH and 10 ml water. Mix with 100 ml water and 10 ml conc. HCl, add 1 drop of KI/KIO_3; titrate against $KMnO_4$ until pink colour persists.

Other reagents for standardization of $KMnO_4$.

•   Anhydrous potassium ferrocyanide, Ferrous ammonium sulfate.

•   Potassium tetraoxalate.

7.7 CERIOMETRY

•   Cerric ammonium sulphate or nitrate is used as powerful oxidising agent, it oxidizes others and it itself gets reduced.

•   It is used only in acidic conditions because in neutral or basic conditions cerric hydroxide precipitates.

•   Standard solutions have intense yellow colour. Under hot conditions it can be used as a self indicator, but at RT, it becomes difficult to notice transformation from faint yellow to colourless.

Reduction reaction

$$Ce^{+4} + c^- \rightleftharpoons Ce^{+3}$$
Yellow   Colourless
cerric   cerrous

Advantages over KMnO$_4$

1.   0.1N solutions are not intensely dark to affect meniscus reading and detection of undissolved solid.

2.   Equivalent weight is equal to molecular weight at all pH, so molar solutions are equal to normal solutions.

3.   Versatile and therefore can be used in all determinations.

4.   Very stable over long period. No effect of light or even heating for a short time on stability.

Various indicators like N-phenylanthranic acid, ferroin, 5, 6 dimethyl ferroin are used for detection of end point.

0.1M Ceric ammonium sulphate preparation as per IP 2014

Dissolve 65 g with gentle heat in mixture of 30 ml H_2SO_4 and 500 ml H_2O. Cool, filter if turbid, dilute with water up to 1000 ml.

Standardisation

Take 0.2g As_2O_3, dried at 105° for 1 hour in a 500 ml conical flask, wash down inner walls with 25 ml 8% NaOH. Dissolve in 100 ml H_2O, mix and add 30 ml. dil. H_2SO_4 and 0.15 ml osmic acid solution. Add 0.1 ml ferroin sulfate solution and titrate till pink solution becomes very pale blue.

1 ml of 0.1M Ceric ammonium sulphate $\approx$ 0.004946 g of As_2O_3.

7.8 TITRATIONS WITH POTASSIUM DICHROMATE

- It is commonly used as an oxidising agent.

- It is very toxic in nature and must be handled and disposed carefully.

$$
\begin{array}{ccc}
O & & O \\
\| & & \| \\
KO - Cr - O - Cr - OK \\
\| & & \| \\
O & & O
\end{array}
$$

$$K_2Cr_2O_7$$

- It is used for oxidation of alcohols and can also be used to distinguish between primary, secondary and tertiary (1°, 2° and 3°) alcohols.

- In the acidified medium it is reduced by consuming 6 electrons.

$$Cr_2O_7^{2-} + 14H^+ + 6e^- \rightarrow 2Cr^{3+} + 7H_2O$$

- Primary alcohols form aldehydes and acids upon oxidation.

$$3CH_3CH_2OH + Cr_2O_7^{2-} + 8H^+ \rightarrow 3CH_3CHO + 2Cr^{3+} + 7H_2O$$

    Alcohol   Aldehyde

$$3CH_3CH_2OH + 2Cr_2O_7^{2-} + 16H^+ \rightarrow 3CH_3COOH + 4Cr^{3+} + 11H_2O$$

Alcohol   Acid

- Secondary alcohols form ketones and tertiary alcohols do not undergo oxidation.

- When alcohols are treated with excess of $K_2Cr_2O_7$, the unreacted dichromate is determined by adding KI producing iodine which will be titrated against sodium thiosulfate using starch as indicator.

$$Cr_2O_7^{2-} + 14H^+ + 6I^- \rightarrow 2Cr^{3+} + 3I_2 + 7H_2O$$

$$2S_2O_3^{2-} + I_2 \rightarrow S_4O_6^{2-} + 2I^-$$

- $K_2Cr_2O_7$ is an excellent oxidant for determination of iron, with indicators such as diphenylamine, diphelylbenzidine.

$$Cr_2O_7^{2-} + 6Fe^{2+} + 14H^+ \rightarrow 2Cr^{3+} + 6Fe^{3+} + 7H_2O$$

- $K_2Cr_2O_7$ is a less powerful oxidant than $KMnO_4$, it does need indicator but has several advantages like

   (i) Available in high purity, can be used as primary standard, need not be standardised.

   (ii) Solutions are stable.

   (iii) Reacts quantitatively with known stoichiometry.

   (iv) Reaction is fast and produces well defined end point.

7.9 TITRATIONS WITH IODINE

Iodimetry

   I_2 is a mild oxidising agent itself undergoing reduction to form iodide.

$$I_2 + 2e \xrightleftharpoons{\text{Reduction}} 2I^-$$

Iodine is volatile, practically insoluble in water. Its redox potential is 0.535 V

   When substances are determined by their direct titration with iodine [arsenite, thiosulfate] the process is called as **iodimetry**.

$$2Na_2S_2O_3 + I_2 \rightarrow Na_2S_4O_6 + 2NaI$$

Oxidized form of thiosulfate

   Indicator starch is added at the beginning of titration. It is colourless, when analyte is completely reacted with iodine, extra drop of iodine reacts with starch to give blue colour.

Iodometry

   Here, iodine liberated in the chemical reaction is titrated against standard thiosulfate.

- I_2 can be generated when HI [HCl/H_2SO_4 with KI] undergoes oxidation.

$$2KI + H_2SO_4 \rightarrow K_2SO_4 + 2HI \quad / \quad KI + HCl \rightarrow KCl + HI$$

$$2HI \underset{}{\overset{\text{Oxidation}}{\rightleftharpoons}} I_2 + 2H^+ + 2e^-$$

- So oxidation of KI in acidic solution generates free I_2 which is titrated with standard sodium thiosulfate. Sodium thiosulfate [reducing agent] again converts free iodine to iodide, so iodometry is used for quantitative estimation of oxidising and reducing agents.

- Starch is used as indicator which forms blue colour with free iodine.

- Method is sensitive and accurate.

Conditions required for Iodometry

1. As redox potential for $I_2/2I^-$ is low, reaction is reversible and does not go to completion.

2. I_2 is volatile, so cold condition is used, moreover starch is less sensitive at elevated temperature.

3. In strongly alkaline solutions, hypoiodide is formed which is a strong oxidising agent.

$$2\,NaOH + I_2 \rightarrow NaOI + NaI + H_2O$$

4. If reaction results in the formation of H^+ ion, they must be removed to ensure completion of reaction.

$$HCO_3^- + H^+ \rightarrow H_2CO_3 \rightarrow H_2O + CO_2 \uparrow$$

5. As solubility of I_2 is low in water, considerable excess of KI must be used.

$$KI + I_2 \rightarrow KI_3$$

6. Despite large of amount KI and acid, rate of oxidation of I^- is too low, hence sufficient time must be given for reaction.

7. Reaction mixture must be kept in a dark place to avoid acceleration of side reaction by light.

$$4I^- + 4H^+ + O_2 \rightarrow 2I_2 + 2H_2O$$

End point detection in Iodometry

1. Iodine itself imparts colour after its release, sensitivity can be increased by adding starch as indicator. In presence of iodide, starch adsorbs iodine to give blue colour.

2. Partitoning of iodine in water-immiscible organic solvent [$CHCl_3$ or CCl_4] can be done, iodine gets easily partitioned by shaking the mixture, violet colour appears due to complex formation between iodine and organic solvent.

Applications

1. Standardisation of thiosulfate solutions.

2. Determination of dissolved oxygen in water by 'Winkler method'.

3. Determination of metals Ba^{2+}, Sr^{2+}, Pb^{2+} which form insoluble chromates for the determination of which iodide is added in excess.

4. Organic compounds like thiols can be determined when excess iodine is added.

Difference between Iodimetry and Iodometry

Iodimetry	Iodometry
1. This is direct titration of substances against standard iodine.	1. This is indirect titration of substances against liberated iodine. This I_2 is further titrated against sodium thiosulfate.
2. It is generally used for determination of reducing agents.	2. It can be used for determination of oxidising and reducing agents.
3. Reaction involved Conversion of iodine to iodide. $I_2 + 2e^- \rightleftharpoons 2I^-$	3. Reaction involved Step 1: Liberation of iodine $2KI \rightarrow I_2 + 2e^-$ Step 2: Reaction of liberated iodine. $I_2 \rightarrow 2I^- + 2e^-$
4. Starch is used as indicator which can be added at the beginning of titration when iodine is present in burette.	4. Starch used as indicator has to be added towards the end point.
5. End point is from colourless to blue.	5. End point is from blue to colourless.

6. No specific requirement of pH, generally performed in acidic pH.	6. It should be performed in pH - weakly acidic or neutral
	In strongly acidic pH.
	Thiosulfate $\rightarrow$ Sulphur
	        decomposition
	In Basic pH
	    I_2 disproportionates and forms hypoiodide and $Na_2S_2O_3$ oxidises to sulfate.

Iodimetry	Iodometry
7. Applications: It is used for estimation of halogens, oxyhalogens, cupric ions and peroxides.	7. It is used for estimation of sulfite, hydroperoxides, thiosulfates, arsenites.
8. Example: Assay of iodine. Standardisation of iodine. Assay of ascorbic acid.	8. Example: Standardisation of sodium thiosulfate. Assay of copper sulfate.

0.05 M Iodine Preparation as per Indian Pharmacopoeia

Dissolve 14g of I_2 in 36g of KI, add 3 drops of HCl, dilute up to 100 ml with water.

Standardisation

Take 0.15g of As_2O_3 in 20 ml of 1M NaOH [warm if necessary]. Add 40 ml of H_2O and 0.1 ml methyl orange solution followed by dil. HCl until yellow colour turns to pink. Add 2g Na_2CO_3 and 50 ml H_2O, 3 ml starch solution. Titrate until permanent blue colour is obtained. Store in amber coloured, glass stoppered bottles. 1 ml of 0.05 m I_2 ≈ 0.004946 g of As_2O_3.

Methyl orange is red at acidic pH and turns yellow at alkaline pH.

•   Assay of iodine – 0.2 I_2 + 1g KI + 2 ml water + 1 ml 2M acetic acid ⁺ 50 ml water, titrate vs. 0.1M $Na_2S_2O_3$ using starch indicator added towards end point (end point is from Blue to colourless).

1 ml of 0.1 M $Na_2S_2O_3$ ≅ 0.01269 g of iodine.

Give Reasons

1.   KI is added in assay of iodine.

Assay of iodine involves solubilisation of iodine in water. Iodine is practically insoluble in water but with KI it forms triiodide complex which is freely soluble in water.

$$KI + I_2 \rightarrow I_3^- + K^+$$

2.   Starch is added towards end point in assay of I_2.

Iodine and starch forms a complex which is blue in colour. Free iodine is brown in colour and starch is white in colour. In any titration which involves addition of starch to solution which contains iodine [as such or liberated in iodometry] starch has to be added towards end point.

During titration, as iodine is present in the flask, starch forms blue colour with it, after end point i.e. when all free iodine has reacted with titrant, extra drops of titrant breaks iodine - starch complex to release free indicator. As complex is broken solution becomes colourless. So expected end point is blue → colourless. However, for this to take place, the complex of starch iodine must be broken, which means that this complex formation should be reversible.

This reaction is reversible only when I_2 is present in low concentration,

I_2 + Starch $\rightleftharpoons$ Blue complex

Colourless

But at the beginning I_2 is present in high concentration, so reaction is irreversible.

I_2 + Starch $\longrightarrow$ Blue complex

So if starch is added at beginning it forms blue complex with I_2 which does not break and hence solution will remain blue colour even after end point, colour change is not observed at end point.

This problem will not be encountered during titration when I_2 is present in burette (Iodimetry), which is added dropwise to analyte containing starch as indicator. As it is added dropwise, I_2 concentration is low and reaction is reversible. Starch can be added in beginning. e.g. standardisation of I_2.

7.10 TITRATIONS WITH PERIODIC ACID (IODIC VII ACID)

Periodic acid is the highest oxo acid of iodine and used as oxidising agent.

Orthoperiodic acid
$[H_5IO_6]$

Metaperiodic acid
$[HIO_4]$

*   Here Iodine exists in oxidation state VII.

*   Like perchloric acid, it can also be used for acid base neutralisation reactions.

*   In redox reactions, periodic acid is used for oxidation of 1, 2 glycols e.g. ethylene glycol, glycerol.

$$CH_2OH$$
$$|$$
$$CHOH + 2HIO_4 \rightarrow 2CH_2O + HCOOH + H_2O + 2HIO_3$$
$$|$$
$$CH_2OH$$

$$(CHOH)_n + (n + 1)\ NaH_4IO_6 \rightarrow 2HCHO + nHCOOH + (n + 1)\ NaIO_3$$

Sodium salt of periodic acid $+ (2n + 1)\ H_2O \cdot CH_2OH$

All such methods involve initial reaction of glycols with excess of periodic acid, followed by determination of excess of periodic acid. After initial reaction gets completed (i.e. oxidation of glycol), KI is added because of which periodic acid liberates iodine (iodometry).

$$2H_5IO_6 + 14KI + 7H_2SO_4 \rightarrow 7K_2SO_4 + 12H_2O + 8I_2$$

$$2S_2O_3^{2-} + I_2 \rightarrow S_4O_6^{2-} + 2I^-$$

- Liberated iodine is titrated against sodium thiosulfate using starch as indicator.

- Blank titration needs to be performed.

- Glycerol can be determined in presence of other glycols, even simple alcohols and phenols do not interfere in oxidation reaction.

Periodic acid solution is not stable in water. It can be standardised using arsenious acid in neutral/slightly alkaline medium back titrating with sodium thiosulphate by iodometry.

$$H_4IO_6Na + H_3AsO_3 + 2OH^- \rightarrow IO_3^- + HAsO_4^{2-} + 4H_2O$$

7.11 TITRATIONS WITH POTASSIUM BROMATE/BROMATOMETRY

- Potassium bromate is a powerful oxidising agent which itself gets reduced to Br$^-$.

$$BrO_3^- + 6H^+ + 6e^- \rightarrow Br^- + 3H_2O$$

At the end of the titration, free bromine gets generated.

$$BrO_3^- + 5Br^- + 6H^+ \rightarrow 3Br_2 + 3H_2O$$

Free bromine has yellow colour, but indicators like methyl orange, methyl red, naphthalene black 12B can be used.

- These indicators retain their colour in acid solution but are rendered colourless by Br$_2$; therefore colour change is observed at end point.

- Most of the time, premature destruction of indicator takes place, requiring additional indicator near point.

- Titration must be carried out slowly to detect colour change.

    Irreversible indicators: Xylidene ponceau, fuchsine, naphthalene black 12B.

    Colour changes to colourless.

    Reversible indicators: 1 naphthoflavone, p-ethoxychrysoidin.

- Applications: It can be used for the determination of As III, Antimony III. Substances which cannot be oxidised directly with $KBrO_3$, but react quantitatively with excess of bromine can also be determined. But as bromine is volatile, titration must be conducted at low temperature and with stoppered containers.

- Excess of bromine is determined with excess of KI and titration of liberated iodine with standard thiosulphate solution.

Preparation of 0.02M KBrO₃

Dissolve 3.34g of $KBrO_3$ in 1 litre of water.

Oxidations with Potassium iodate/Iodatometric titrations

Potassium iodate is a strong oxidising agent in particular reaction conditions.

1. With iodide ion, in acidic conditions it generates iodine.

$$IO_3^- + 5I^- + 6H^+ \rightarrow 3I_2 + 3H_2O$$

2. With more powerful reductants, iodate reduces to iodide.

$$IO_3^- + 6Ti^{3+} + 6H^+ \rightarrow I^- + 6Ti^{3+} + 3H_2O$$

Thus under suitable conditions, it reacts quantitatively to form both iodide and iodine. Iodate titrations can be performed in the presence of alcohol, saturated organic acids and many other kinds of organic solvents.

Applications

1. Determination of percentage of KI.

2. Assay of weak iodine solution.

3. Assay of aqueous iodine solution.

7.12 TITANOUS CHLORIDE TITRATIONS

Titanous chloride is a good reducing agent widely used for reduction of azo, nitro, nitroso compounds. These colourants reduce to colourless compounds, when titrated with titanous chloride and thus this titration is used for determination of strength of dyes. Titanium (Ti^{3+}) oxidises itself to Ti^{4+}

$$R - NO_2 + 6H^+ + 6Ti^{3+} \rightarrow R - NH_2 + 2H_2O + 6Ti^{4+}$$

Care should be taken to exclude all oxygen from the flask during titration by purging the system with CO_2 or N_2, because it can lead to oxidation of Ti^{3+}.

Internal indicators which reduce after reduction of sample can be used to detect end point. e.g. light green SF, alizarin etc. or addition of excess of titrant and then back titration of such excess with suitable dye like methylene blue can be done.

Preparation and standardisation of 0.1 N TiCl₃ as per IP 2014.

Dilute 100 ml of TiCl₃ solution with 200 ml of HCl and add sufficient freshly boiled and cooled water to produce 1000 ml. Standardise by titrating with it 25 ml of 0.1 M ferric ammonium sulphate acidified with H_2SO_4 using ammonium thiocyanate as indicator.

1 ml of 0.1M ferric ammonium sulphate ≈ 0.01543 g of TiCl₃.

Alternative procedure for preparation of 0.1N TiCl₃

Add 500 ml of HCl and 500 ml of 20% TiCl₃ to 7 litres of plastic bottle containing 5 litres of DW. Dilute to 7 litres with water.

Storage: It should be stored under inert gas and restandardised at least weekly.

Assay of Indigo Carmine

Indigo Carmine

0.5 g indigo carmine + 15 g sodium hydrogen tartarate monohydrate + 200 ml water.

Boil with stream of CO_2 and titrate hot solution with 0.1 M TiCl₃ until colour changes from blue through yellow to orange.

1 ml of 0.1 M TiCl₃ ≅ 23.31 mg of indigo carmine.

7.13 SODIUM NITRITE (NaNO₂) TITRATIONS

Sodium nitrite is used as titrant in determination of primary aromatic amines. If a substance does not contain primary aromatic amino group, but can form it by some reaction then also NaNO₂ titration can be used. e.g. Paracetamol.

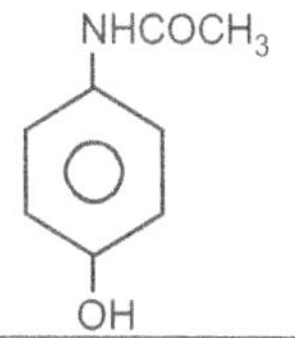

NHCOCH$_3$

OH

It does not contain primary aromatic amino group, however after reflux with acid it hydrolyses to primary amine.

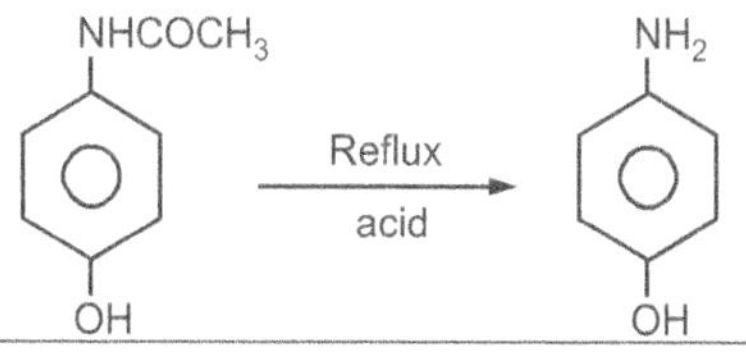

NHCOCH$_3$ NH$_2$

$\xrightarrow[\text{acid}]{\text{Reflux}}$

OH   OH

Now it can be determined with NaNO$_2$.

NaNO$_2$ in acidic condition forms nitrous acid.

$$NaNO_2 + HCl \rightleftharpoons HNO_2 + NaCl$$

Sodium   Nitrous
nitrite   acid

Nitrous acid in presence of HCl reacts with 1° aromatic amino group to form dizonium salt.

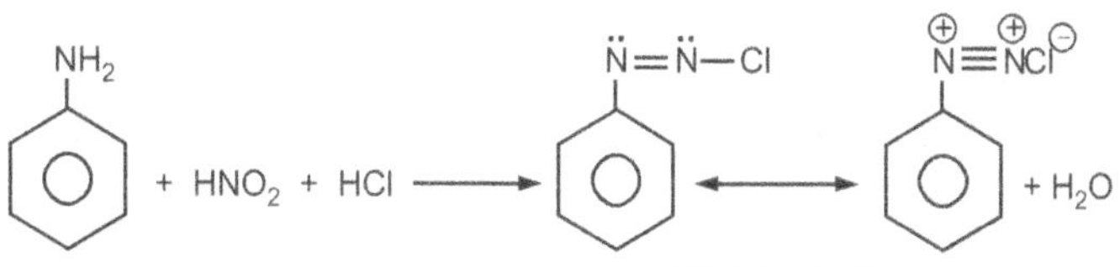

NH$_2$

+ HNO$_2$ + HCl $\longrightarrow$ N=N—Cl $\longleftrightarrow$ N≡NCl + H$_2$O

Dizonium salts

As dizonium salt contains two nitrogens, it is very unstable at room temperature and tends to loose N$_2$ in the gaseous form. To prevent this decomposition of reaction product, reaction is carried out under ice cold conditions [0-5°C].

End point of sodium nitrite titrations is determined by detecting excess of nitrous acid, because when all of analyte reacts completely, extra drop of NaNO$_2$ falls in solution to form HNO$_2$ which remains unreacted.

7.28

Therefore, at the end point, a drop of solution is removed and placed on starch iodide paper. Starch iodide paper contains starch and KI. Analyte solution contains HNO_2, HCl.

$$KI + HCl \rightarrow HI + KCl$$

$$2HI + 2HNO_2 \rightarrow I_2 + 2NO + 2H_2O$$

$$I_2 + Starch \rightarrow Blue\ colour$$

This is example of an external indicator.

Precautions in Sodium Nitrite Titrations

1. Maintain reaction at 0-5°C to prevent decomposition of dizonium salt.

2. Perform slow titration with continuous stirring and allow atleast 1 min. between addition of titrant.

    As temperature is low during titration, reaction becomes slow.

3. Maintain excess of HCl in titration.

    HCl is required in three stages.

    (a) Formation of HNO_2.

    (b) Formation of dizonium salt.

    (c) Detection of end point.

    Hence strong HCl [2M HCl] is used generally and in excess.

4. Formation of spontaneous blue colour on paper is taken as end point.

    Due to air oxidation, iodide converts to iodine and paper may turn blue slowly before end point. This is not true end point. Excess of HNO_2 releases iodine immediately giving spontaneous blue colour, this is true end point.

    With these precautions, $NaNO_2$ titrations can be performed. These titrations can also be performed with potentiometric end point detection.

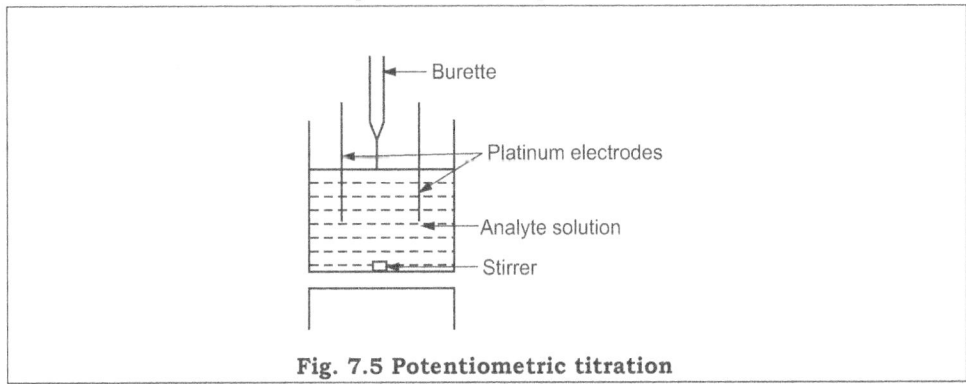

Fig. 7.5 Potentiometric titration

During titration, addition of titrant causes deflection in galvanometer needle and again comes back to original position. At the end point, both electrodes becomes depolarised and permanent deflection is observed.

Preparation and standardisation of 0.1 M NaNO$_2$ as per IP 2014.

Preparation: 7.5 g NaNO$_2$ $\xrightarrow{\text{Water}}$ 1000 ml

Standardisation: 0.3 g sulphanilamide + 50 ml 2M HCl + 3g KBr → Cool in ice bath → Titrate with prepared 0.1 M NaNO$_2$ determining end point potentiometrically. 1 ml of 0.1 M sodium nitrite ≅ 0.01732 g of sulfanilic acid.

2.   **Assay of sulphanilamide [as per European pharmacopoeia]**

0.140 g of sulphanilamide + 50 ml dil. HCl + 3g KBr, cool in ice bath and titrate slowly with 0.1 M NaNO$_2$ determining end point potentiometrically.

Sulphanilamide   Dizonium salt

1 ml of 0.1 M NaNO$_2$ ≅ 17.22 mg of sulphanilamide.

7.14 PHARMACEUTICAL ASSAYS BY REDOX TITRATIONS AS PER OFFICIAL BOOKS

1.   **Ferrous sulphate IP 2014**

Dissolve 2.5 g of NaHCO$_3$ in a mixture of 150 ml of water and 10 ml of H$_2$SO$_4$. When effervescence ceases, add about 0.5 g of sample [ferrous sulphate], shake to dissolve it and titrate with 0.1 M ceric ammonium nitrate using 0.1 ml of ferroin solution as indicator, until red colour disappears.

1 ml of 0.1 M ceric ammonium nitrate ≅ 0.02780 g of FeSO$_4$ · 7H$_2$O.

2. Ascorbic acid IP 2014

Weigh accurately about 0.1 g of sample and dissolve it in a mixture of 100 ml of freshly boiled and cooled water and 25 ml of 1M H_2SO_4. Immediately titrate with 0.05 M Iodine, using starch solution as indicator until a persistent blue-violet colour is obtained.

1 ml of 0.05 M Iodine $\cong$ 0.008806 g of ascorbic acid.

3. Ascorbic acid tablets IP 2014

Weigh and powder 20 tablets. Weigh accurately a quantity of the powder containing about 0.15 g of ascorbic acid and dissolve as completely as possible in a mixture of 30 ml and water and 20 ml of 1M H_2SO_4. Titrate with 0.1 M cerric ammonium sulphate using ferroin sulphate solution as indicator.

1 ml of 0.1 M cerric ammonium sulphate $\cong$ 0.008806 g of ascorbic acid.

Have you heard about him?

Walther Hermann Nernst (25 June 1864-18 November 1941) was a German physicist who is known for his theories behind the calculation of chemical affinity as embodied in the third law of thermodynamics, for which he won the Nobel Prize in chemistry in 1920.

He joined Wilhelm Ostwald at Leipzig University where Vant hoff and Arrhenius were already established and it was in this distinguished company of physical chemists that Nernst began his important researches.

Nernst helped to establish the modern field of physical chemistry and contributed to electrochemistry, thermodynamics and solid state physics.

He is also known for developing the Nernst equation. When Nernst was developing his third law, he read a paper of Einstein on the quantum mechanics of specific heats at cryogenic temperatures and was so impressed that he traveled all the way to Zurich to visit him in person.

Einstein's status changed dramatically after Nernst's visit. He was relatively unknown in Zurich in 1909, and people said "Einstein must be a clever fellow if the great Nernst comes all the way from Berlin to Zurich to talk to him".

Nernst helped Einstein to get his dream job, A named professorship at the top university in Germany, without teaching duties, leaving him free to do research.

8

GRAVIMETRIC METHODS

8.1 Introduction

8.2 Unit Operations in Gravimetry

8.3 Applications

8.1 INTRODUCTION

Gravimetry is the technique of 'Analysis by weight'. It is a process of isolating and weighing an element in pure form of definite composition either by precipitation, volatilisation or electroanalytical method.

Unlike other methods of analysis, gravimetry involves detection of element from its compound. e.g. Mg^{2+} in $MgSO_4$, Al^{3+} in alum.

Isolation of element can be achieved either by–

(i) Precipitation: It is conversion of analyte to sparingly soluble precipitate, which is subsequently filtered, washed and dried.

e.g. Ammonium oxalate as precipitating agent for Ca to form Ca oxalate.

(ii) Volatilisation: Compound is allowed to be ignited or heated so that element of interest is separated from its compound.

(iii) Electroanalytical methods: Element is allowed to deposit on electrode by virtue of its charges. No filtration is required.

(iv) Thermal methods

Out of these, precipitation is the most simple popular method. Formation of coarse crystalline precipitate is desirable in gravimetry.

To the sample solution of analyte, precipitating agent is added slowly, with continuous stirring. Gravimetric analysis by precipitation is accurate, simple and inexpensive method of analysis if careful steps are taken to minimise potential interferences.

8.2 UNIT OPERATIONS IN GRAVIMETRY

Gravimetric analysis involves the following steps to be followed in a sequence.

1. Sampling
2. Dissolution/Preparation of solution
3. Precipitation
4. Testing completeness of precipitation
5. Digestion/Ageing of precipitate
6. Filtration
7. Washing
8. Drying/Ignition
9. Weighing
10. Calculation

1. Sampling

From the bulk, uniform and homogeneous sample which is representative must be taken. Quantity of sample must be small. If it is available in powder form, it is preferred because of ease of weighing. Factors which affect sampling are cost of test, value of product, end use of product, accuracy of method and nature of the material.

2. Dissolution/Preparation of solution

Sample collected must be dissolved in a suitable solvent to get a clear solution. Conditions must be maintained to have low solubility of precipitate and suitable form for filtration. Accordingly temperature, pH, volume of solution, concentration of other constituents must be maintained. The solution must be heated on a water bath or asbestos gauze to the desired temperature. Steps can be taken to remove interfering substances.

3. Precipitation

(i) Theory of Precipitation/Gravimetry

- Precipitation obtained by crystal growth is most desired as it gives coarse crystalline precipitate.

There are two phases involved

(i) Nucleation: Here molecules in solution come together randomly and form small aggregates.

(ii) Particle growth: Addition of molecules to nucleus to form crystal.

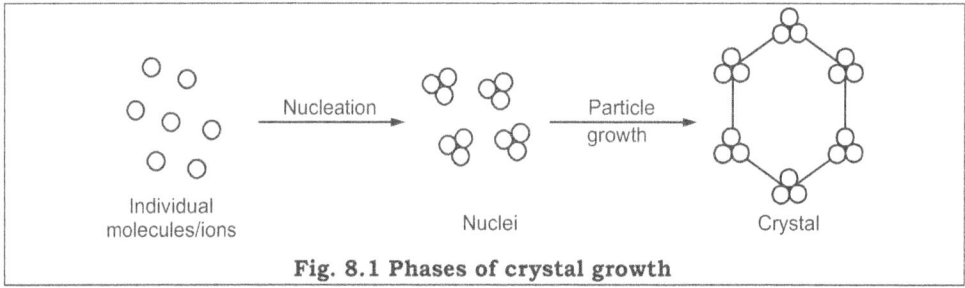

Fig. 8.1 Phases of crystal growth

- Nucleation and particle growth always compete for molecules/ions being precipitated.

  If nucleation is faster than particle growth-large number of small aggregates occur giving colloidal suspensions.

  If particle growth is faster than nucleation, only a few, large particles form giving pure crystals.

  This rate of nucleation and particle growth depends on amount of precipitation solute present. It is described by a quantity known as relative supersaturation (RS).

Von Weimarn equation/Ratio

$$RS = \frac{Q - S}{S} \tag{1}$$

When Q – S is high → colloidal precipitate is obtained.

When Q – S is small → crystalline precipitate is obtained.

$$\text{Particle size of precipitate} \propto \frac{1}{\text{Relative supersaturation}}$$

RS = Relative supersaturation (concentration of mixed reagent before precipitation)

Q = Actual concentration of solute added to the solution

S = Concentration of solute in solution at Equilibrium (solubility)

As particle size is inversely proportional to relative supersaturation for formation of coarse precipitate [more particle size] relative supersaturation must be less.

As

$$RS = \frac{Q - S}{S}$$

For RS to be less, 'Q' should be small and 'S' should be high.

(i)   So solubility must be high and therefore hot solution [elevated temperature increases solubility] must be used.

(ii) For Q (concentration to be precipitated] to be small, dilute solution must be used and reagent added slowly with constant stirring.

Each precipitate is characterised by solubility product,

e.g. $[Pb^{2+}]\ [SO_4^{2-}]\ =\ 2.2 \times 10^{-8}$

When product of concentration of both lead and sulphate ions exceed solubility product, precipitation will occur.This solubility product changes with temperature, pH and solvent used.

Conditions to get coarse crystalline precipitate

1.   Precipitating agent must be added slowly with constant stirring.
2.   Precipitation must be carried out in dilute solution.
3.   Precipitation must be carried out in hot solution if precipitate is stable.
4.   Digestion must be carried out for long time.
5.   The precipitate must be washed with dilute solution of electrolyte and not with water because it will lead to peptisation.
6.   If co-precipitation occurs, then it should be dissolved and reprecipitated .

Types of Precipitates

1.   **Crystalline:** Have definite shape.
2.   **Curdy:** Aggregate of small porous molecules.
3.   **Gelatinous:** Jelly like particles.

Ideal precipitate must be coarse, crystalline in nature, having low solubility, must have less adsorption sites and should be converted completely to easily weighable form.

These properties can be summarised as-

1.   Precipitate must be less soluble/insoluble in solvent employed. Therefore, there is no loss in filtration and washing.
2.   It should get easily filtered.
3.   Physical nature of precipitate [size] must be unaffected by washing.
4.   Precipitate must be stable to experimental and environmental conditions.
5.   It should be convertible to pure compound of definite composition.

(ii) Precipitating agents

A number of reagents are available which act as precipitating agents.

Selective precipitating agents: Such agents react with a particular class of compounds and form precipitate.

Specific precipitating agent: Such agents react with specific substances and form precipitate.

• Precipitating agent can be added or generated in the solution by a chemical reaction (in situ).

e.g. ethyl oxalate, sulfamic acid.

Sulfamic acid acts as insitu precipitating agent generating sulphate ion.

$$HSO_3NH_2 + H_2O \rightarrow H^+ + SO_4^{2-} + NH_4^+$$

Sulfanic   Precipitating

acid   agent

Precipitating agents

Organic agents   Inorganic agents

Chelating/   Ion association
complexing   precipitants
agents

Fig 8.2: Precipitating Agents

A. Organic agents

They are more selective than inorganic agents. They form precipitates with varying solubility in water.

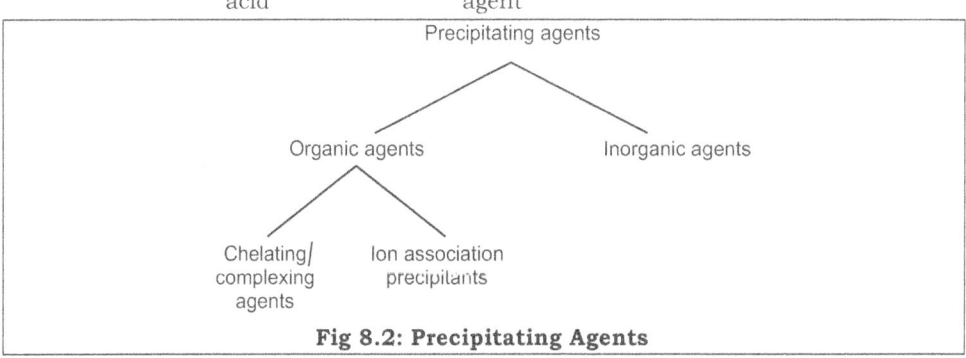

8 Hydroxy Quinolive

Dimethyl glyxomine

e.g. 8 hydroxy quinoline [oxine] for Al^{3+}, Mg^{2+}. Anthranilic acid for Na^+

Dimethyl glyxomine for Ni^{2+}, Pd^{2+}

B. Inorganic agents

They are not very selective. They form slightly soluble salts or hydroxides.

e.g. HCl - Ag^+, Hg^{2+}

H_2SO_4 - Ba^{2+}, Pb^{2+}, Sr^{2-}

NH_4SCN – Cu^{2+}.

C. Chelating/Complexing agents

They form co-ordination compounds. They donate a pair of electrons and form a ring with metal ions. They are weak acids and pH must be maintained by use of a suitable buffer during precipitation.

Products are generally non-polar and have low solubility in water [high solubility in organic solvents] are highly coloured and have low densities.

D. Ion association precipitants

These agents ionize in aqueous solutions to form cations/anions which react with oppositely charged species to give slightly soluble substances. They form ionic bond and does not form ring like complexing agents.

$$\begin{array}{l} \text{COOH} \qquad\qquad\qquad \text{COONa} \\ | \qquad\qquad\qquad\qquad\quad | \\ \text{COOH} + 2NaHCO_3 \rightarrow \text{COONa} + 2H_2O + 2CO_2 \end{array}$$

e.g. Oxalic acid for Ca^{++}, Mg^{++}, Na^+, Sodium tetraphebnyl boron for K^+

Tetraphenylarsonium for $2[C_6H_5]_4As^+$

Table 8.1: Organic precipitants

No.	Name	Str.	Metals precipitated
1.	Dimethyl glyoxime	$CH_3 - C = NOH$ $\quad\quad\;\; \|$ $CH_3 - C = NOH$	Ni^{2+}, Pd^{2+}
2.	8 Hydroxyquinoline (oxine)		Al^{3+}, Mg^{2+}, many other metals like Cu^{2+}
3.	α Benzoin oxime (Cupron)		Cu^{2+}, Mo^{3+}
4.	Sodium diethyl dithiocarbonate	$\qquad\quad S$ $\qquad\quad \|\|$ $(C_2H_5)_2\, N - C - S^- + Na^+$	Many metals from acid solution

(iii) Purity of precipitate/sources of contamination of precipitate.

Precipitate must be as pure as possible. It may get contaminated by two processes namely Co and post precipitation.

Table 8.2: Differences between Co-precipitation and Post precipitation

Co-precipitation	Post precipitation
1. Simultaneous precipitation of substances which would otherwise not precipitate if the analyte had been absent. It occurs at the time main precipitation.	1. When precipitate is allowed to stand in presence of mother liquor, some impurities get precipitated. It occurs after main precipitation.
2. This is precipitation of extraneous matter which is not generally precipitated under general condition by precipitant used.	2. This is precipitation of substances which have common ion with primary precipitate.
3. e.g. $BaCl_2$ + $KMnO_4$ + H_2SO_4 Impurity $\rightarrow BaSO_4$ $BaSO_4$ precipitate appears violet coloured because of $KMnO_4$.	3. e.g. CaC_2O_4 + $MgSO_4$ Impurity $\rightarrow MgC_2O_4$ + $CaSO_4$
4. It may occur through several mechanisms and therefore it has four types. (a) Surface adsorption (b) Occlusion (c) Mixed crystal formation (d) Mechanical entrapment	4. There are no further types.
5. Extent of contamination decreases with increase in time of contact of solution with mother liquor.	5. Extent of contamination increases with increase in time of contact of solution with mother liquor.
6. Extent of contamination decreases with faster agitation of solution by mechanical or thermal means.	6. Extent of contamination increases with faster agitation of solution by mechanical or thermal means.
7. Extent of contamination is smaller than post precipitation.	7. Extent of contamination is greater than co-precipitation.

Mechanisms/Types of Co-precipitation

a. Surface adsorption

It is surface phenomenon, hence proportional to surface area. Ions which forms less soluble salt gets adsorbed on surface of ion precipitate which is more soluble. e.g. Ca^{2+} (salt) adsorbs on surface of Mg^{2+} salt.

Process is reversible [desorption] i.e. passage of adsorbed ion from surface of precipitate into the solution is possible.

Equilibrium depends on **1.Concentration:** It is directly proportional to adsorption.

2. **Temperature:** It is inversely proportional to adsorption. High temperature favours desorption.

3. **Nature of adsorbed ion:** Common ion and oppositely charged ion gets adsorbed.

4. **Conditions:** pH, concentration, temperature affect adsorption.

5. **Area of surface:** It is directly proportional to adsorption.

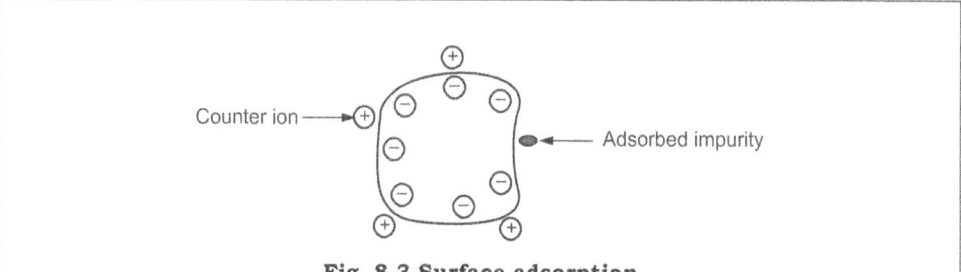

Fig. 8.3 Surface adsorption

b. Occlusion

Trapping of foreign ion within the walls of crystals during rapid growth of crystal is occlusion. Therefore, rate of precipitation should be low. Amount of contamination is very high when impurity is isomorphous or forms solid solution.

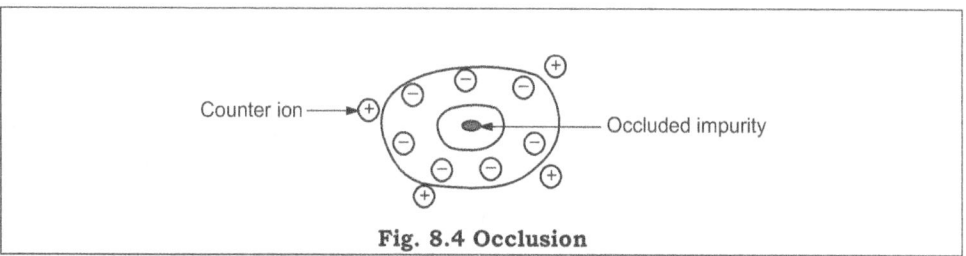

Fig. 8.4 Occlusion

c. **Mixed crystal formation/Isomorphous replacement**

One ion of crystal lattice of solid is replaced by foreign ion. e.g. Precipitation of $BaSO_4$ in presence of lead, mixed crystal of Ba and lead sulphate gets formed. It depends on ratio of analyte and contaminant ion.

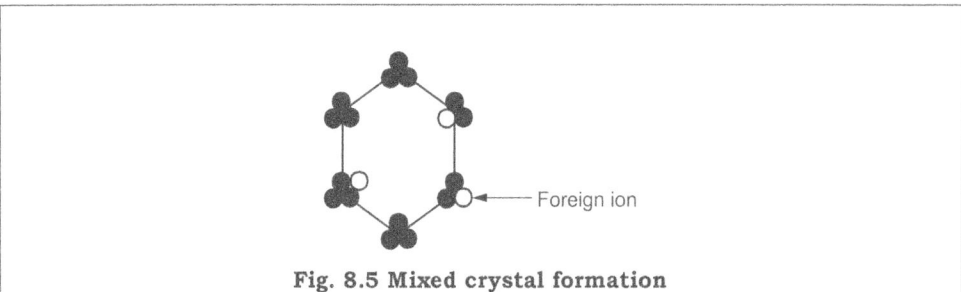

Fig. 8.5 Mixed crystal formation

d. **Mechanical entrapment**

During crystal growth, trapping of solution in between crystal is mechanical entrapment. Raising temperature will allow the solution to escape from it.

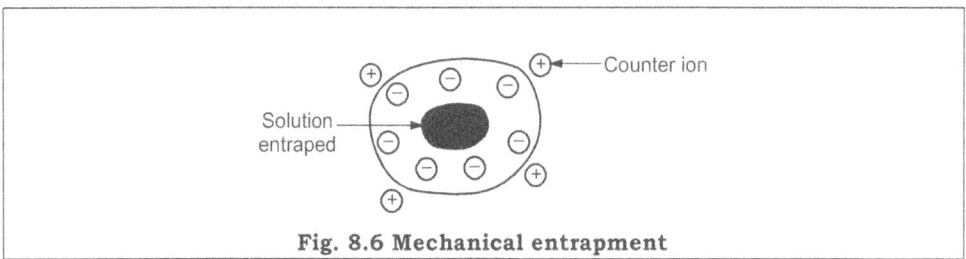

Fig. 8.6 Mechanical entrapment

5. **Testing completeness of precipitation**

Once precipitation has occurred, completeness can be checked by adding more precipitating agent and observing whether precipitating occurs or not. Continue till no further precipitation occurs.

6. **Digestion/Ostwald Ripening**

To increase degree of coarseness of precipitate, it is allowed to stand overnight in contact with mother liquor or heated for sometime till supernatant liquid becomes clear and no further precipitation occurs. If precipitate is soluble in hot solution allow it to cool and then filter. It is done to get larger and more pure crystals because small crystals are not desirable in gravimetry as they have higher surface energy and higher apparent solubility than large crystals.

- When precipitate is allowed to stand in presence of mother liquor [solution from which it was precipitated] large crystals grow, small particles tend to dissolve and reprecipitate on surface of larger crystals. In addition, individual particles agglomerate to efficiently share a common counterion layer and agglomerated particles finally cement together by forming connecting bridges.

- It decreases surface area, imperfections disappear and release adsorbed or trapped impurities into solution.

- It improves filterability and purity. It can be performed at room temperature or at elevated temperature to speed up the process.

7. Filtration

- Separation of precipitate from mother liquor is achieved by filtration.

Following filter media are available.

1. **Filter papers:** These are semi-permeable paper barriers placed perpendicular to a liquid or air flow and are suitable for buchner funnel. They are made up of cellulose and those with low ash content are typically suitable for gravimetry. Circular filter papers with different diameter and porosities are available, accordingly they are denoted by different numbers. Porosity control flow rate and particle retention.

Table 8.3: Types of Filter Papers and their Properties

Filter paper grade	Thickness (μm)	Porosity	Flowrate	Particle retention
No. 50	200	Fine	Slow	2.7 μm
No. 40	210	Medium	Medium	8 μm
No. 41	220	Coarse	Fast	20-25 μm
No. 42	200	Fine	Slow	2.5 μm

- Ash content is determined by ignition of cellulose filter at 900°C in air.

- Selected filter paper must be cut to the appropriate size of the funnel.

- Size of paper/funnel shall be based on bulk of precipitate and not on volume to be filtered.

2. **Filter pulp/slurry**

- They are typically used for filtration of gelatinous and very fine precipitates which clog the filter paper.

- It is prepared by macerating filter paper pieces with hot distilled water or commercially filter pulp tablets are available which swell upon mixing with water.

- Such pulp is added to solution containing precipitate and stirred. Precipitate gets occluded within filter pulp. This mixture is filtered to obtain precipitate embedded within filter pulp.

- Separated mass is heated subsequently, so paper used for preparing pulp also has to be ash less.

- Addition of pulp/slurry also facilitates retention of precipitate on filter paper, cleaning of beaker in which precipitation was carried out.

- Volume of the pulp shall be equal to the bulk of precipitate to ensure complete occlusion.

3. Filter crucibles

- In cases where precipitate reacts with cellulose and where filter paper is not stable at temperatures required for drying, filtration is carried out in filter crucibles. Such crucibles may have filter mats specially prepared and inserted on perforated base or filter discs permanently fused in the body of crucible. They are very convenient to collect precipitate directly in a vessel which can be dried and weighed.

(a) **Filter mats:** Earliest crucibles containing filter mats were Gooch crucibles containing mat of purified asbestos supported in platinum crucible.

Silica and porcelain crucibles were also made available in this way. All such crucibles were known as Gooch crucibles.

  - Platinum Gooch crucibles are very resistant to chemicals, heating and can be used for rapid filtration of fine particles named as munroe crucibles.

  - Glass fibre discs made up from fine borosilicate glass are also available in place of asbestos mat. They are also resistant to chemical attack and can be heated upto 500°C.

  - Permanent filter discs are used nowadays, because of their fixed assembly. They are of following types. They are available in tall, narrow and small, wide shapes.

Table 8.4: Types of Permanent Filter Discs

	Sintered glass	Silica	Porcelain
Composition	Pyrex glass with sintered ground glass disc fused in it	Fused silica [quartz/ vilriol]	Glazed porcelain
Types	G_1, G_2, G_3, G_4 ↓ ↓ Coarse Fine	G_1, G_2, G_3, G_4	---
Suitable for Heating up to	200°C	1000°C	Not to be heated directly on flame
Resistance	Resistant to chemicals	Resistant to chemicals but affected by phosphates, alkalies, HF withstand sudden heating and cooling	Costly and susceptible for cracking

Filter paper

Filter pulp

Crucibles

8. Washing

For purification of precipitate it is filtered. Co-precipitated impurities [on surface] can be removed by washing. Precipitate which is wet with mother liquor can also be washed to remove mother liquor.

Many precipitates cannot be washed with pure water, peptisation may occur [this is reverse of coagulation]. Hence, washing can be done with solution of electrolytes. But that electrolyte must be volatile at the temperature to be used for drying/ignition and must not dissolve the precipitate.

In precipitation, coagulated particles have a neutral layer of adsorbed primary and counterions. Washing with another electrolyte causes counterion to be forced into closer contact with the primary layer and promotes coagulation. Washing with water dilutes and removes foreign ions, counterion will occupy larger volume, with more solvent molecules between it and the primary layer. This is called as peptisation.

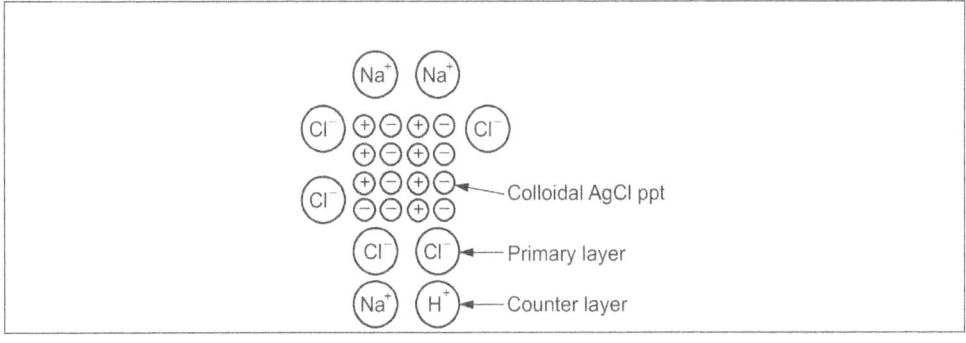

As a result the repulsive forces between particles becomes strong again and particles revert back to colloidal state and pass through filter. It can be prevented by adding electrolyte to washing solution. Washing must be given till filtrate becomes colourless. Check for completion of washing must be carried out.

9. Drying or Ignition of precipitate

If the collected precipitate is in a form suitable for weighing, it must be heated to remove water and adsorbed electrolyte from the wash liquid.

Drying – Heating at temperature up to 250°C.

Ignition – Heating at temperatures higher than 250°C and below 1200°C.

Ignition is required when precipitate must be converted to a more suitable form for weighing.

e.g. $$MgNH_4PO_4 \xrightarrow[900°C]{Ignition} Mg_2P_2O_7$$

| Magnesium ammonium phosphate | Mg pyrophosphate |

Drying shall be done to constant, reproducible weight. It can be achieved by repeated alternate drying/heating and cooling of product till a constant weight is observed within 0.3 mg.

10. Weighing

Dried precipitate must be weighed until constant weight is obtained.

11. Calculation

% analyte can be determined by formula

$$\% \, A = \frac{\text{Weight of analyte}}{\text{Weight of sample}} \times 100$$

$$\% \, A = \frac{\text{Weight of precipitate} \times \text{Gravimetric factor}}{\text{Weight of sample}} \times 100$$

$$\text{Gravimetric factor} = \frac{\text{Formal weight of analyte (g/mol)}}{\text{Formal weight of precipitate (g/mol)}}$$

$$\times \frac{a \ \text{mol analyte}}{b \ \text{mol precipitate}}$$

8.3 APPLICATIONS

1. It is precise and accurate method of analysis for many substances particularly inorganic ions.

Substance analysed	Precipitate formed	Precipitate weighed	Interferences
Fe^{3+}	$Fe(OH)_3$	Fe_2O_3	Al^{3+}, Ti^{3+}, Cr^{3+}
	Fe cupferrate	Fe_2O_3	Tetravalent metals
Al^{3+}	$Al(OH)_3$	Al_2O_3	Fe^{2+}, Ti^{3+}, Cr^{3+}
Ca^{2+}	CaC_2O_4	$CaCO_3$ or CaO	All except Mg^{2+}
SO_4^{2-}	$BaSO_4$	$BaSO_4$	NO_3^-, PO_4^{3-}, ClO_3^-
Cl^-	AgCl	AgCl	Hg(I)

2.   Routine assays of metallurgical samples are done by gravimetry.

3.   To determine atomic masses of elements up to six decimal places.

4.   Because of high accuracy, it can be used to validate/calibrate other methods/instruments.

5.   Determination of a variety of organic substances like lactose in milk products, salicylates in drug preparations, phenolphthalein in laxatives, nicotine in pesticides, cholesterol in cereals and benzaldehydes in almond extracts.

6.   For verifying the composition of standard reference materials.

Have you heard about him?

Frank Austen Gooch (May 2, 1852 – August 12, 1929) was a chemist and engineer. Gooch is known for invention of the Gooch crucible, which is used for filtration, Born in Watertown, Massachusetts, Gooch was a Professor of Chemistry at Yale University from 1885 to 1918. He was awarded Ph. D., by Harvard University in 1877.

He devised or perfected a large number of analytical processes and methods, including the Gooch filtering crucible, quantitative separation of lithium from the other alkali metals, the estimation of boric acid by distillation with methanol and fixation by calcium oxide, method development for estimating molybdenum, vanadium, selenium, and tellurium, studies on the use of the paratungstate and pyrophosphate ions in analysis.

The analytical methods devised by Gooch reflect as a rule his own practical turn of mind. He sought whenever possible to avoid costly apparatus and time-consuming procedure, and often obtained the desired results by devices of exceptional simplicity.

He was a man of real culture, with broad interests and a keen appreciation of the finer things of life; he was ready and interesting in conversation, and a most delightful companion. He was gifted with an exceptionally keen sense of humor, loved to hear a good story or to tell one, he was fond of chess, and of music.

GLOSSARY

- **Agitation:** It is brisk stirring of a liquid.
- **Amplification:** The operation which makes analytical signal stronger.
- **Analyte:** It is a substance or chemical constituent that is of interest in an analytical procedure.
- **Anions:** These are the atoms or radicals or group of atoms, that have gained electron's to become negatively charged.
- **AR (analytical reagent):** It is a chemical of high enough purity that it is suitable for analytical laboratory procedures.
- **Back titration:** It is a titration done in reverse; instead of directly titrating the original sample, a known excess of titrant is added to the analyte solution, and the excess is back titrated verses another titrant.
- **Calibration:** It's a process to determine, check, or rectify the graduation of any instrument giving quantitative measurements.
- **Cations:** These are the atoms or groups of atoms that have lost electron/s to become positively charged.
- **Coefficient of thermal/cubic expansion:** It describes how the size of an object changes with the change in temperature.
- **Colligative properties:** These are properties of solutions that depend upon the ratio of the number of solute particles to the number of solvent molecules in a solution, and not on the type of chemical species present.
- **Colloidal precipitate:** It consists of solid particles with dimensions that are less than 10^{-4} cm.
- **Common ion effect:** It is responsible for the reduction in the solubility of an ionic precipitate when a soluble compound combining one of the ions of the precipitate is added to the solution which is in equilibrium with the precipitate. It states that if the concentration of any one of the ions is increased, then ions in excess should combine with the oppositely charged ions.

- **Conductometry:** It is a measurement of electrolytic conductivity to monitor a progress of chemical reaction

- **Decant:** Process of gradually pouring (liquid) from one container into another, typically in order to separate out sediment.

- **Decomposition:** It is the process by which organic substances are broken down into a much simpler form of matter.

- **Degrees of freedom:** It is the number of values in the final calculation of a statistic that are free to vary. It is usually one value less than total number of observations.

- **Dependent variable:** It is the variable measured in the experiment and the one affected during the experiment.

- **Dilution:** It is the process of reducing the concentration of a chemical by increasing volume of solution with addition of solvent.

- **Dissociation:** It is a process in which molecules (or ionic compounds such as salts, or complexes) separate or split into smaller particles such as atoms, ions or radicals, usually in a reversible manner.

- **Electrode:** It is a solid electric conductor through which an electric current enters or leaves an electrolytic cell or other medium.

- **Endpoint:** It is the point actually measured in titration, a physical change in the solution as determined by an indicator or an instrument.

- **Equivalence point:** It is the theoretical completion of the reaction. It is the volume of added titrant at which the number of moles of titrant is equal to the number of moles of analyte, or some multiple thereof.

- **High-Performance Thin-Layer Chromatography (HPTLC):** It is the advanced form of TLC and comprises of the use of chromatographic layers of utmost separation efficiency and the employment of instrumentation for all steps in the procedure like precise sample application, standardized reproducible chromatogram development and software controlled evaluation.

- **High-performance liquid chromatography (HPLC):** It is a technique used in analytical chemistry used to separate the components in a mixture, to identify each component, and to quantify each component.

- **HPLC grade:** These solvents are glass distilled; submicron filtered and they undergo rigorous specification testing to provide lot-to-lot consistency.

- **Ignition:** It is exothermic chemical reaction between a fuel and an oxidant accompanied by the production of heat and conversion of chemical species.

- **Impurities:** These are the substances inside a confined amount of liquid, gas, or solid, which differ from the chemical composition of the material or compound.

- **Independent variable:** It is the variable that is varied or manipulated by the researcher.

- **Inflection point:** It is a point on a curve at which the sign of the curvature (i.e., the concavity) changes. Inflection points may be stationary points, but are not local maxima or local minima.

- **Internal standard:** It is a chemical substance that is added in a constant amount to the samples, blank and calibration standards in a chemical analysis. It is chemically similar to analytc but gives different signal.

- **Interpretation:** It is the action of explaining the meaning of something.

- **Ionization:** It is the process by which an atom or a molecule acquires a negative or positive charge by gaining or losing electrons to form ions, often in conjunction with other chemical changes.

- **Infrared spectroscopy (IR):** It is the spectroscopy that deals with the infrared region of the electromagnetic spectrum.

- **Isolation:** It is the separation of the chemical entity in pure form from the matrix.

- **Isotope:** One of two or more atoms that have the same atomic number (the same number of protons) but a different mass number (different number of neutrons).

- **Law of mass action:** The rate of any chemical reaction is proportional to the product of the masses of the reacting substances, with each mass raised to a power equal to the coefficient that occurs in the chemical equation.

- **Le Châtelier's principle:** When a system at equilibrium is subjected to change in concentration, temperature, volume, or pressure, then the system readjusts itself to (partially) counteract the effect of the applied change and a new equilibrium is established.

- **Linear relationship:** In this relationship any given change in an independent variable will always produce a corresponding change in the dependent variable

- **Sample**: It is a subset from a larger population that researcher collects and analyzes to make inferences about population.

- **LR grade (Laboratory grade):** These are the chemicals that meet minimum purity standard and are usually acceptable for experiments and demonstrations which do not require quantitative results.

- **Mass spectrometry (MS)** is an analytical technique that helps to identify the amount and types of chemicals present in a sample by measuring the mass-to-charge ratio and abundance of gas-phase ions.

- **Meniscus:** It is the curve in the upper or lower surface of a liquid close to the surface of the container usually burette.

- **Mother liquor:** It is the part of a solution that is left over after crystallization, or the solution from which crystallization was carried out.

- **Neutralization:** It is a chemical reaction in which an acid and a base react quantitatively with each other.

- **Nuclear magnetic resonance (NMR):** It is a physical phenomenon in which nuclei in a magnetic field absorb and re-emit electromagnetic radiation.

- **Occlusion:** It is the process in which adsorbed impurity is physically trapped inside the crystal as it grows.

- **Peptization:** It is the process responsible for the formation of stable dispersion of colloidal particles in dispersion medium. It is opposite to coagulation.

- **Population:** It is a collection of people, items, or events about which researcher makes inferences.

- **Potentiometry:** It is a method used in electroanalytical chemistry, usually to find the concentration of a solute in solution. In potentiometric measurements, the potential between two electrodes is measured using a high impedance voltmeter.

- **Purging:** It is a process of displacing the air with an inert gas.

- **Qualitative:** These are the descriptions or distinctions that are based on some quality or characteristic rather than on some quantity or measured value.

- **Quantitative:** These are the descriptions or distinctions that are based on some quantity or measured value.

- **Radioactivity:** It is the process by which a nucleus of an unstable atom loses energy by emitting ionizing radiation.

- **Reduction potential:** It is a measure of the tendency of a chemical species to acquire electrons and thereby getting reduced. Reduction potential is measured in volts (V), or millivolts (mV).

- **Reference standard:** It is a standardized substance which is used as a measurement base for similar substances.

- **Reflux:** It is a distillation technique involving the condensation of vapors and the return of this condensate to the system from which it was originated.

- **Refractometry:** It is a technique that measures how light is refracted when it passes through a given substance.

- **Scattering:** It is a general physical process where some forms of radiation, such as light, sound, or moving particles, are forced to deviate from a straight trajectory by one or more paths due to localized non-uniformities in the medium through which they pass.

- **Solubility:** It is the property of a solid, liquid, or gaseous chemical substance called solute to dissolve in a solid, liquid, or gaseous solvent to form a homogeneous solution of the solute in the solvent.

- **SOP (Standard Operating Procedure):** It is a document which describes the detailed procedure of regularly recurring operations relevant to the investigation.

- **Spectroscopy:** It is the study of the interaction between matter and radiant energy.

- **Spiking:** It is the process of addition of sample or impurity to the standard.

- **Standard electrode potential:** It is the measure of individual potential of a reversible electrode at standard state, which is with solutes at an effective concentration of 1 mol dm^{-3}, and gases at a pressure of 1 atm.

- **Standardization:** It is the process of determining the exact concentration.

- **Supersaturated solution:** It is the solution that contains more solute, or dissolved material, than it would contain under normal conditions.

- **Titrant:** It is the solution involved or used in a titration to determine the concentration of an unknown solution.

- **Titration curve:** It is a curve in the plane whose x axis is the volume of titrant added since the beginning of the titration, and whose y axis is the concentration of the analyte or its response at the corresponding stage of the titration.

- **Titration:** It is the slow addition of one solution of a known concentration (called a titrant) to a known volume of another solution of unknown concentration until the reaction reaches neutralization, which is often indicated by a color change.

- **Turbidity:** It is a measure of solution clarity and amount of the material suspended in solution which decreases the passage of light through the solution.

- **Valence (or valency):** It is a measure of combining power of element with other atoms when it forms chemical compounds or molecules.

- **Validation:** It is a documentary evidence which gives a high degree assurance that a particular process, equipment, utility consistently performs the specified function and meets its pre determined standards and quality attributes.

- **Volatilisation:** It is the process whereby a dissolved sample is vapourised.

BIBLIOGRAPHY

1. **A Textbook of Pharmaceutical Analysis** by Connors KA, 4/Ed., John Wiley & Sons, New York.
2. **Analytical Chemistry** by Christian GD, 6/Ed., John Wiley & Sons, New York.
3. **Analytical chemistry**, problems and solutions by Khopkar SM, New Age International Publishers, New Delhi.
4. **Fundamentals of Analytical Chemistry** by Skoog, West, Holler and Harvest, 8/Ed., Thomson, Ghaziabad.
5. ICH, **Text on Validation of Analytical Procedures**: Text and Methodology, Q2 (R1), International Conference on Harmonization of Technical Requirements for Registration of Pharmaceutical for Human Use. Geneva, 2005.
6. **Indian Pharmacopoeia**, 2014, The Indian Pharmacopoeia Commission, Ltd. New Delhi.
7. **Pharmaceutical Analysis** by Higuchi, Reprint 2004, CBS Publisher & Distributors, New Delhi.
8. **Pharmaceutical Analysis** by Parimoo P, CBS Publishers and Distributors, New Delhi.
9. **Pharmaceutical Analysis** by Kasture AV, Mahadik KR, Wadodkar SG and More HN, Vol. II, Nirali Prakashan, Pune.
10. **Pharmaceutical Drug Analysis** by Kar A, First Print, 2001, Minerva Press, New Delhi.
11. **Pharmaceutical Statistics**, **Practical and Clinical Applications** by Bolton S and Bon C, 5/Ed., Vol 135, Marcel Dekker, New York.
12. **Practical Pharmaceutical Chemistry** Part-I by Beckett AH and Stenlake JB, 4/Ed., CBS Publisher & Distributors, New Delhi.
13. **Quantitative Analysis** by Day RA and Underwood AL 5/Ed., Prentice Hall of India Pvt Ltd, New Delhi.
14. **Quantitative Analysis** by Alexyev V, Student Edition, CBS Publisher & Distributors, New Delhi.
15. **The Quantitative Analysis** of Drugs by Garrat DC, 3/Ed., CBS Publisher & Distributors, New Delhi.
16. **U.S. Pharmacopoeia** 30/ NF25, U.S. Pharmacopoeial Convention, Rockville, MD.
17. **Vogel's Text Book of Quantitative Chemical Analysis** by Mendham J, Denney RC, Barnes JD and Thomas MJK, 6/Ed., Pearson Education, New Delhi.

✱✱✱

INDEX

www.ingramcontent.com/pod-product-compliance
Lightning Source LLC
Chambersburg PA
CBHW080731020726
47503CB00010B/2876